CHASING DREAMS

TIMBER RIDGE RIDERS
∽ Book Five ∾

CHASING DREAMS

Maggie Dana

PAGEWORKS PRESS

#5

ISBN 978-0-9851504-4-0

Edited by Judith Cardanha
Cover by Margaret Sunter
Interior design by Anne Honeywood
Published by Pageworks Press
Text set in Sabon

~ TO ALL HORSE LOVERS ~

keep chasing those dreams

1

ON HER FIRST DAY at Winfield High School, Kate McGregor was called into the principal's office. She'd just figured out which locker was hers when the PA system announced her name. Its stentorian tone made it sound like she'd committed an unpardonable sin.

"Yikes," Kate said. "Am I in trouble?"

"Don't be an idiot," said her best friend, Holly Chapman. "You've only been here five minutes. That's not enough time for *me* to get in trouble, never mind you." She shook out her blond pony tail and tied it up again, then hefted her purple backpack onto one shoulder. "I'll see you at lunch, okay?"

"Yeah," Kate said, gritting her teeth.

Had she pulled a ninth-grade faux pas, like wearing the wrong color socks or taking a shortcut over the school's tiny front lawn? The sign said *Keep Off the Grass*, but there was no grass to keep off of. It had shriveled into sisal. Besides, Holly and the others had run across it, and they weren't being summoned into Mrs. Gordon's office.

Kate knocked on the principal's door.

"Come in," Mrs. Gordon said. She flashed Kate a toothy smile, waved her into a chair, and opened a blue folder. "It says here you'll be leaving Vermont at Thanksgiving. Is that right?"

"Yes," Kate said, wishing it wasn't. "I'm going back to Connecticut when my father gets home from Brazil."

"Professor Benjamin McGregor?" the principal said.

On the bookshelf behind her was a display case filled with dead butterflies. Amid the rainbow of colors, Kate recognized a rare blue morphos, three African swallowtails, and a painted lady. Two yellow moths trapped inside a glass pyramid sat beside a pot of paper clips on Mrs. Gordon's desk.

Kate nodded. "Yes, that's him."

Not many people knew about her dad, unless they obsessed over butterflies the way he did. He wrote obscure books about them and taught entomology at the University of Connecticut. If a critter had compound eyes, fuzzy legs, and colorful wings, he was all over it. People, not so much.

Mrs. Gordon picked up her paperweight.

"Besides being the principal, I also teach biology," she said, stroking the glass as if it were a pet. "I'm hoping your father might be willing to come and give my students a talk about his research. Do you think he would?"

Kate let out her breath, unaware she'd been holding it. So that's what all this fuss was about. She hadn't broken some arcane school rule.

"I'll write and ask him," she said.

But it probably wouldn't do much good. Her father was deep in the Amazon, cataloging rare species. He had patchy cell phone service and no Internet connection. The best way to reach him was via airmail, but that took weeks and weeks to get there. Kate figured jungle drums were more reliable. Faster, too.

"Thank you," Mrs. Gordon said, flashing another toothy smile. "You can join your class now. Algebra, isn't it?" She ran a hand through her frizzy black hair. Bits of it stuck out behind her ears like bat wings. "I hope you'll be happy here."

"I will," Kate said, smiling back.

She'd just had the best summer of her life, living at Timber Ridge with Holly and her mom, Liz, who ran the riding stable. If Kate's father hadn't decided to stay in Brazil for another three months, they'd be back on the UConn campus by now. Their tiny condo didn't have enough room for a hamster, never mind a horse, and that was Kate's biggest problem.

Two months ago, she'd rescued a horse.

Everyone told her she was nuts, but Tapestry—her scruffy chestnut mare—had turned into a showstopper. The previous weekend they'd outjumped their rivals to help Timber Ridge win team gold at the season's largest horse show.

Eager to share the news with her dad, Kate had tried his cell phone. To her surprise, the call had gone though, but the connection was so bad that they'd had to shout at one another. She'd already written to him about Tapestry and sent photos, but her letters never arrived.

She explained as best she could.

"Well done," her father said, sounding proud. "But I'm not sure about your horse. We'll talk about it when I get home. Things have changed at UConn, and I might not be—"

The line had gone dead.

Kate tried to reach him again and again, but her calls didn't even get to Dad's voicemail. His inbox was full.

No surprise there.

When he was home, he couldn't even remember to empty the dishwasher, never mind his phone's inbox. Kate loved her father, but his haphazard approach to modern life drove her nuts.

* * *

To Kate's relief, she was up to speed in algebra, and her English teacher assigned a couple of books she'd already read and loved. Even biology wasn't a problem. They'd be studying, of all things, endangered butterflies and moths.

She knew all about those.

At lunchtime, she found the cafeteria, filled a tray with food, and joined Holly at her table. The whole riding team was there, except for Angela Dean and her cousin Courtney. They were probably being treated to lunch by Mrs. Dean at the fanciest restaurant in town. Kate dug into her vegetable lasagna.

"So, what did The Gorgon want?" Holly said.

Kate looked up. "Who?"

"Our wild and woolly principal," said Sue Piretti.

Sue gave a huge grin and fluffed out her sandy red hair. Her parents ran the Timber Ridge ski area. Her brother, Brad, was an extreme snowboarder. He knew all about wild and woolly.

Robin Shapiro shook her head, and her mop of brown curls danced about like demented Slinkies. "Mrs. Gordon's not too bad, once you get to know her."

"She's nice," Kate said. "I liked her."

"But what did she want?" asked Jennifer West.

Today, Jennifer's hair had purple streaks that

matched her sparkly eye shadow and frosted nail polish. She owned a chestnut gelding named Rebel who jumped like a kangaroo and loved to eat vanilla pudding. Jennifer was English, and she'd invited Kate and Holly to spend next summer in England at the equestrian center owned by her grandmother, an Olympic rider.

Kate shrugged. "Just some stuff about my dad."

"Phew," Holly said. "I thought for sure you were being hung, drawn, and quartered."

"Or beheaded," said Sue.

"How about boiled in oil?" Jennifer said. "Or—"

"C'mon guys," Robin said, glancing at the clock. "We've got five minutes to get back to class."

Kate shot her a thankful look.

Robin was just like her mother. Mrs. Shapiro was the voice of reason on the Timber Ridge Homeowners' Association. Whenever Mrs. Dean got out of line, Robin's mom shot her down ... nicely, of course.

Outside the gym, Kate spotted Angela and Courtney amid a group of cheerleaders. They carried green-and-yellow pom-poms and wore short green skirts with yellow stripes. They looked sleek and impossibly glamorous.

Kate pulled on her wool cap and crammed in as much of her hair as possible. It was half blond and half brown—a bleaching experiment that backfired—and

Kate despised it. But Holly insisted the two-tone effect was wicked cool. She said it complemented Kate's green eyes and made her look like an exotic feline. The trouble was, she'd said it in front of Angela.

Feeling like a nerd in her stupid hat, Kate forced herself to look straight ahead. *Don't make eye contact. Pretend they're not there.*

"Meow," Angela said, flexing her crimson claws.

Courtney giggled. "Here, kitty kitty."

The two cousins were reverse images of one another. Both had icy blue eyes and long, straight hair, but Angela's was jet black and Courtney's was the color of corn silk. They whispered to the other girls as Kate walked by, but she managed to ignore them.

Angela Dean was the only person Kate wouldn't miss when she left Timber Ridge. Ever since her arrival, Angela had pulled one nasty trick after another in her campaign to evict Kate from the barn. She'd even spread rumors on Facebook that Kate's mare was stolen property.

* * *

For the next three weeks, Kate juggled homework and barn chores with riding Tapestry and trying to contact her father. It was like he'd dropped off the face of the earth. She e-mailed his colleagues at UConn, but they

7

told her not to worry. Professor McGregor was in a remote tribal village. He would get in touch as soon as he returned to civilization.

"Why don't they send in a helicopter?" Holly said.

"Or the Marines?" said Sue.

Kate laughed them off and pretended she wasn't concerned. Her father had been in worse places before, including Sumatra when the tsunami hit. He'd spent many days helping rescue survivors.

He finally called on a Friday afternoon when Kate was about to leave her study hall. She heaved a sigh of relief, then almost choked when he told her he'd be home the third week in October.

A month sooner than expected.

His department at UConn had been downsized, but he'd been offered a new position at the University of Wyoming. It was big horse country out there, he'd said. They'd be able to afford a small house with a barn and enough land for Tapestry.

"That's cool, I guess," Holly said, when Kate found her in the library, prepping for a biology quiz. "At least you get to keep her."

"I know," Kate wailed. "But Wyoming? That's, like, two thousand miles away." She didn't want to move, not even to a state that had herds of wild horses.

"Maybe he'll find a job in California instead," Holly

said. She gave a wistful sigh. "I'd love to live in Hollywood."

"I wouldn't," Kate said. "It's full of movie stars."

"Including Nathan Crane," Holly said, rolling her eyes. "He's your boyfriend, remember? He lives in Beverly Hills."

"Except he's hardly ever there," Kate said.

Right now, Nathan was on location in New Zealand for the movie *Moonlight*. Part of it had been shot at the stables, and Kate had ridden as a stunt double for Tess O'Donnell, the film's female star. Adam, Holly's boyfriend, had been Nathan's double. Adam and Nathan gone to school together in Vermont. When Kate first met Nathan, she didn't know who he was, and Holly still loved to tease her about it.

"I wish you could stay here forever," Holly said.

Kate sighed. "Me too."

It was her wildest dream, but it could never come true. Her father needed a big research university with plenty of funds to support an entomologist who loved butterflies.

"Couldn't your dad get a job in Vermont?" Holly said "We've got lots of colleges here." She brightened. "We've even got a butterfly museum. I went with my third-grade class. Maybe he could—"

Sadly, Kate shook her head. Dad was an absent-minded professor from the tips of his unruly hair to the soles of his dilapidated deck shoes. She couldn't imagine him shepherding kids through a fake jungle filled with captive butterflies and moths.

Holly sighed. "I hate biology," she said, staring morosely at a diagram of a frog.

"Why?"

"Because we have to dissect animals."

Kate said, "Frogs hardly count."

"Oh, yes they do. They've got feelings, just like us," Holly said, her bright blue eyes still focused on the frog.

"Just be glad you don't have to cut up a horse," Kate said, wincing as she remembered how close Tapestry had come to being inside a can of dog food.

Holly closed her textbook. "Have you heard about Sue's Halloween party?"

"Yeah," Kate said. "They're going trick-or-treating on horseback. Jennifer's making a zombie costume for Rebel."

"You make it sound like you're not coming," Holly said.

Kate shrugged. "I probably won't be here." Dad's plans were all over the place, and Kate had no idea where she'd be at the end of October.

"How about the Spruce Hill hunter pace?"

"When is it?" Kate said.

"The weekend before Halloween."

"I guess so," Kate said. "I've never ridden in one before. What's it like?"

"It's kind of like a cross-country course," Holly said, as they left the school library. "But the jumps are much lower, and there's always a way around them."

"Does the fastest rider win?"

"Nuh, uh. It's a hunter *pace*, not a hunter *race*," Holly said. "They send a rider over the course before-hand to set the time and pace. The pair of riders that comes closest to the set time is the winner."

"Pair?" Kate said.

"Yup. Mom said she's going to have us pull our riding partner's name out of a hat."

"Why can't we choose our own?" Kate said, leading the way toward their lockers. "I want to ride with you and Magician."

Holly shrugged. "I guess Mom decided this is the fairest way. She's got six riders, and you know that nobody will want to ride with Angela."

"Ugh," Kate said. "I hope I don't get her."

Poor Liz. It wasn't easy having Angela on the riding team. But with her overbearing mother as president of the Homeowners' Association, Liz didn't have a choice. Mrs. Dean insisted that Angela be included in all team events, never mind if she qualified or not.

"Did you know that Marcia's been bugging Angela to let her ride Skywalker?" Holly said.

Kate stared at her in astonishment. Marcia was Angela's younger sister. She was a pretty good rider for a kid her age, but she'd never be able to handle a horse like Skywalker. "He's way too much for her."

"That's what Mom keeps telling her," Holly said. "But Marcia won't listen. She's driving Mom crazy."

"So why doesn't Mrs. Dean get Marcia a horse?" Kate said. "They've got pots of money."

Holly pulled a face. "I know, but Angela's her favorite. I bet she's told her mother that Marcia doesn't deserve a horse of her own."

"Angela doesn't deserve one either." Kate shoved old homework papers into her locker. "She hasn't ridden Skywalker since the Labor Day show."

"I wish she wasn't back on our team," Holly said. "I wish she'd stayed with Larchwood."

"Then Adam would be stuck with her," Kate said.

Holly's boyfriend rode for Larchwood Equestrian Center, Timber Ridge's biggest rival. Two days before the last show, Angela had dropped out of the Timber Ridge team and joined Larchwood at the last minute. Kate had narrowly beaten her in the junior jumping, and Holly had soundly beaten her in equitation.

"She's a spoiled bratface," Holly said. "I just hope I don't pull her name out of the hat." She gave a rueful grin. "Maybe we'll get lucky and end up riding together, huh?"

"Keep your fingers crossed," Kate said.

"I bet Angela can't wait for the hunter pace," Holly said. "It'll be her last chance to prove she can ride better than you."

Kate knew Holly was right. "Is there any way to cheat?"

"On a hunter pace?"

"Yes."

"I've no idea," Holly said, slamming her locker shut. "But if there is, Angela will figure it out."

2

Lost in thought, Kate sat beside Holly as their school bus labored up the hill toward Timber Ridge. Holly was talking a mile a minute with Sue and Jennifer, excited about the hunter pace and Sue's plans for her Halloween party.

"Have you invited Angela and Courtney?" Holly said.

Sue shook her head violently. "No way."

The girls cheered—Angela wasn't on the bus; neither was her cousin—and Kate turned to look out the window. She'd get to compete in the hunter pace, but she'd miss Sue's party.

Dad had called again. He would drive up to watch Kate ride, and afterward he'd stop for a quick visit with his sister in the village before going back to Connecticut.

This made Kate feel a bit guilty. She hadn't been to see Aunt Marion in weeks. The following Friday, Dad said, Kate would join him in Wyoming so they could look at houses together.

Then he'd dropped a bombshell.

It made no sense, he said, to truck Tapestry all the way out west when Wyoming had so many great horses. Kate could sell her and buy a much better one out there.

Gloomily, Kate rubbed a clear spot on her dirty window. Timber Ridge Mountain towered above them. Its ski trails were still a rich, dark green, but in just a few weeks, they'd be covered in white. Sue had told them her father and his crew were already setting up the pipes and snow guns that would ensure good skiing by Halloween.

The bus took a sharp right and entered Timber Ridge Manor. Clustered at the base of the mountain, the group of elegant homes looked like an advertisement for country living at its best. The reproduction Capes and faux colonials swept by, each one surrounded by well-manicured lawns and professional landscaping. Angela Dean's three-story mansion had stone lions guarding its front door.

Beyond it, Kate saw the barn and Holly's house, which wasn't nearly as smart as the others. The bus jolted to a halt, and Kate and Holly got off.

"Let's change and go to the barn," Holly said.

She dumped her backpack on the kitchen table. Horse magazines slid to the floor, taking with them Liz's mug of coffee that she'd abandoned that morning. Kate mopped up the mess, then glanced at the pile of mail.

On top was an invitation to Sue's party.

Kate wished she could go. It wouldn't be much fun without Nathan, but Adam would be there and so would Brad Piretti. He was in tenth grade. According to the high school grapevine, he'd asked about Kate. Was she sticking around or leaving? Gossip about her spread like measles, like she was some sort of freak. One rumor had Kate jetting off to New Zealand to join Nathan Crane; another claimed she was about to head for the jungle to help her father find the world's biggest spider.

"The talk makes you cool and mysterious," Holly insisted.

Kate sighed and slouched into their bedroom. There was nothing mysterious about her or her life. She loved horses and wanted to ride them. Everything else was secondary. Well, except for getting into a good college that would prepare her for a job that provided enough funds for her to ride horses.

She tore off her school clothes and slipped into a pair of old breeches. After shoving her feet into paddock boots, Kate ran out the back door and followed Holly to the barn. Its comforting smell reached her immediately—

fresh hay and horses; the rich aroma of manure. Kate plunged into the barn's dim interior and heard her horse whicker.

It was the best sound in the world.

Tapestry stuck her copper-colored nose over the stall door and whuffled up the carrots Kate offered.

"Good girl," Kate said, patting her neck.

She was exactly the sort of horse Kate had always dreamed of but never expected to own—a golden mare with a flaxen mane and tail, just like the pictures in her favorite book from childhood. Kate slid back the door. With a muffled grunt, Tapestry dropped to her knees, folded her hindquarters, and collapsed onto a bed of clean shavings. She looked up at Kate, clearly hoping for another treat.

Kate burst out laughing.

She'd taught Tapestry this trick after learning about it from an Australian web site. It had taken weeks and weeks of patient work, but Tapestry had finally gotten it. She even trusted Kate enough to let her snuggle. It was like cuddling a giant teddy bear. The younger kids loved it. Armed with carrots, they were always begging Kate to make Tapestry perform.

"Get up, you silly horse," Kate said.

Tapestry lumbered to her feet. Kate wrapped her arms around the mare's warm neck and gave her a hug.

Tapestry nuzzled her pockets, so Kate fed her another carrot.

"You're spoiled rotten," she said.

Holly called from her mother's office. "Mom's ready for us to pick names for the hunter pace," she cried. "Hurry up."

Kate gave her last carrot to Magician, Holly's black gelding. He lived in the stall beside Tapestry and he was Kate's second-favorite horse. She used to ride him all the time, until two months ago when Holly was well enough to start riding him herself.

"Hustle," Holly yelled.

Kate zoomed through Liz's door and almost ran into Angela and Courtney, who were wearing identical pink outfits. Courtney had a tennis racquet tucked beneath one arm; Angela was chewing gum. It didn't look as if she planned to practice for the hunter pace.

"Okay, kids, this is it," Liz said above the babble of excited voices. She picked up a black riding helmet and shook it vigorously.

Yet again, Kate crossed her fingers. It seemed as if that's all she'd been doing lately—hoping for something to turn out the way she wanted.

"How does this work?" Sue asked.

Liz said, "I've put six numbers in the hat. The two

girls who pull out numbers one and two will ride together as a team. Then three and four, and—"

"Five and six," Jennifer finished.

"This had better not take all day," Angela complained. "I want to play tennis."

"Shut up," Holly said. "If you didn't spend so much time whacking a stupid ball around, your horse wouldn't be such a beast. He's been cribbing again. Did you know that? His stall door is bitten to bits."

"Quiet," Liz said. She turned to Sue. "You go first."

With a dramatic groan, Sue closed her green eyes and dipped her hand into the helmet. She drew out a folded sticky note.

"Don't look," Liz said. "Not till everyone's had a turn."

There was only one number left when the helmet reached Kate. As her fingers closed around the last bit of paper, she shuddered. It would be just her luck to draw Angela Dean.

"Okay, you can all look now," Liz said.

"I've got number one," Jennifer said. "Who's number two?"

"Me," Holly yelled.

Kate's heart sank. Maybe she'd get Sue or Robin. Either one would be great.

"Who's got number three?" Liz said.

"I do," Sue said. "And Robin's number four."

Kate didn't even bother to look at her piece of paper. Feeling sick, she stuffed it into her pocket. The worst had happened, and there was nothing she could do about it.

"This is really stupid," Angela said. "I don't want to ride with Kate. Let's do it over."

"Nobody's forcing you to compete," Liz said.

"You can always drop out," Holly said. "You've done it before." She pinned Angela with a look. "Or maybe you'd rather ride for another team."

There was a collective intake of breath. For a mad moment, Kate wished Angela *would* drop out. But that would be even worse—she'd be stuck without a partner and her father wouldn't get to see Tapestry in action.

"I'll ride," Angela snapped, then turned on Kate. "Just don't mess it up for me, that's all. Your horse will never be able to keep up with Skywalker, and you'd better not keep me from winning."

Courtney yawned. "Are we done here yet?"

"Not quite," Liz said, glaring at her. She softened her tone. "Okay, kids, here's the scoop. This hunter pace will be about three miles long, and the jumps won't be any higher than two and a half feet."

"Kids' stuff," Angela said.

"Lucky for you," Holly said. "You'd flub it up if they were any bigger."

Patiently, Liz kept going, and Kate didn't know how she managed to keep her temper. Angela was beyond rude. So was her insufferable mother, and Angela had obviously taken lessons from her. But Liz didn't have much choice. Her job depended on being in Mrs. Dean's good graces.

"There'll be spotters at all the jumps," Liz explained. "One rider in each pair has to jump. You can take turns, or one of you can jump them all. It doesn't matter. You can figure it out as you go along." She paused. "If neither of you jumps, you'll get penalty points."

"Do we gallop the whole way?" Robin said.

Liz smiled. "No, the idea of a hunter pace is to ride at a steady canter or a brisk trot," she said. "Just pretend you're out hunting, and don't race."

Angela examined her fingernails as if they were of the utmost importance. "How do you win this thing?"

"By coming closest to the pacemaker's time."

"What does that mean?" Jennifer said.

Liz sat down at her desk and picked up a piece of paper. "Here's what the rules say: 'The perfect time is predetermined by an official pacesetter. The winning pair will be that pair that completes the course closest to the perfect time.'"

"That sounds really dumb," Angela said. "How can I win if I don't know what time to shoot for?"

"That's all you care about, isn't it?" Holly said. "Winning."

"I've heard enough," Angela said. "I know what to do now." She grabbed her cousin's hand. "Come on. Let's go and play tennis." Arm in arm, they sashayed out of Liz's office.

"Bratface," Holly muttered. "She'll never change."

"That's all right for you to say," Kate said, feeling miserable. "You don't have to ride with her. I'm the one who's stuck."

Holly looked thoughtful for a moment. "It might not be so bad," she said. "You know Angela wants to win, and with you as her partner, she certainly won't do anything to mess up your chances. If she did that, she'd ruin her own."

Kate looked at her in amazement. "Wow, I hadn't thought of that. I hope you're right."

"Of course I am," Holly said. "Come on. Let's get ready to practice. I want to take Magician over the hunt course."

"Wait," Kate said. "I've got another question."

"Okay," Liz said.

"If both riders decide to jump, do they have to do it side by side?"

"The only time you need to be beside your partner is when you go through the start and the finish lines," Liz said. "Other than that, you can ride single file or however you want." She paused. "Kate, this is a fun event, okay? Stop taking it so seriously."

Liz's words stayed with Kate as she ran a brush over Tapestry's golden coat. The hunter pace might be fun for everyone else, but her future was at stake. She had to convince her father that Tapestry was worth trucking all the way out to Wyoming.

Which meant she had to win.

3

EVERYONE EXCEPT ANGELA spent the next ten days practicing for the hunter pace. Liz's riding team jumped the
hunt course, timed one another along the trails, and
argued the best way to ride a perfect hunter pace.

"I'm going to trot the whole way," Sue said, patting
her Appaloosa's spotted neck. "Tara's got a long stride."

Jennifer shook her head. "Cantering is better."

Her chestnut gelding had powerful hindquarters and
he could canter for hours without seeming to get tired.
He was amazingly comfortable, too. Kate had ridden
him a couple of times when Jennifer was on vacation.

"Let's do both," Robin suggested. Her gray mare,
Chantilly, had worked up a sweat, and her dappled coat
had darkened to the color of wet slate.

Holly grinned. "Adam's going to gallop flat-out."

"Boys!" Sue gave a dramatic sigh. "That's what my crazy brother would do, except he'd do it on a snowboard."

"If it gets any colder," Robin said, shivering, "that's what we'll all be doing."

The sky had darkened, so they headed back to the barn. Snow this early in the season wasn't unusual, although the weekend weather was expected to be dry and sunny.

Kate rode beside Holly.

It was Friday afternoon and she hadn't heard from her father since he left the Amazon five days ago. He was supposed to have gotten home yesterday, but so far, not a word. She checked her cell phone again—just an old text from Nathan, but nothing from her dad.

"I can't believe Angela," Holly said, kicking her feet free of the stirrups and swinging her legs back and forth. "She wants to win, but she can't be bothered to practice."

"Has she ever ridden a hunter pace before?" Kate said.

Holly shrugged. "I doubt it."

"Have you?"

"Once," Holly said. "Right before, you know—" Her eyes filled with tears, and she wiped them away.

"Yeah," Kate said. She knew how much Holly hated

to talk about the car accident. It had killed her father and left her in a wheelchair for two years. She'd started riding again only a couple of months ago.

"The ride was great," Holly said. "I didn't win, but I totally stuffed myself on the hunt breakfast afterward." She patted her stomach. "Quiches, scrambled eggs and bacon, a humongous fruit bowl, and hot chocolate with marshmallows."

"Sounds yummy," Kate said.

Holly shoved her feet back in the stirrups. "Mom says the food at this one will be even better. Adam's sure to make a pig of himself."

"Who's he riding with?" Kate said.

"Kristina James," Holly replied. "They won it last year."

"By galloping?"

"No," Holly said. "He's just showing off."

There was an edge to Holly's voice. Was she jealous of Adam's partner? Kristina rode a palomino Quarter Horse and they'd won several ribbons at the show on Labor Day weekend. According to Adam, she'd become quite friendly with Angela and Courtney.

* * *

On Saturday morning, Kate couldn't stop yawning as she groomed Tapestry. She'd been awake half the night worrying her father wouldn't show up and that, if he did, he'd still insist she sell her horse before they moved to Wyoming. Holly said she was crazy. Her father was going to love Tapestry as much as they did.

"Where's Angela?" Kate said, looking around the barn. There was no sign of her hunter pace partner. Had Angela changed her mind? It would be just like her to mess up Kate's plans.

Liz clipped a lead rope to Skywalker's halter and led him out of his stall. "Load him for me, would you? Angela's driving to the hunter pace with Mrs. Dean."

Kate looked at Angela's bay gelding. Marcia had polished him to perfection the night before. Kate thought she was nuts. That was Angela's job, but as Holly pointed out, Marcia was trying to earn brownie points so her mother would buy her a horse.

"Trust Princess Angela to weasel out of doing any work," Holly grumbled as she followed Kate to the horse van. Her arms were full of tack, including Angela's. "It would serve her right if we left her horse at home."

Kate led Skywalker up the ramp.

For once, he loaded easily. It usually took ten minutes and lots of carrots to get him on board. He was calmer, too, without Angela around. She always riled him up.

* * *

An hour later they reached Spruce Hill Farm. It was all decked out for Halloween with pumpkins, corn stalks, and plastic spiders dangling from webs strung along the wooden fence. Witches on broomsticks flew across the barn's roof; ghosts floated above its large double doors.

"Cool," Holly said. "A haunted hunter pace."

"We should've worn our costumes," Jennifer said.

Kate was glad they hadn't. She'd be suffocating in the headless horseman outfit she'd worn at Mrs. Dean's fancy dress party on Labor Day weekend, never mind that she wouldn't be able to see where she was going.

Liz drove her six-horse rig into the parking lot, already filled with trailers from all over New England. Kate recognized the red-and-black Larchwood van. Its riders wore red hoodies; their horses sported red blankets and matching leg wraps. Adam's half-Arabian pinto, Domino, looked especially sharp in his.

The moment they pulled up, Adam waved and ran over to greet them. Holly rolled down her window. Leaning inside, Adam brushed her cheek with a kiss. Holly shrugged as if she didn't care, but her pink face gave her away.

"There's Angela," Robin said, pointing.

She and Courtney were standing by Mrs. Dean's silver Mercedes, talking to a dark-haired boy dressed in gray breeches and a black sweatshirt. He looked familiar to Kate, but she couldn't quite place him.

"That's Derek Thompson," Adam said. "His parents own all this." He waved toward the indoor arena, the riding rings, and the fields beyond.

Holly scowled. "Then I bet he knows the course like the back of his hand," she said. "He's bound to win."

"Not this time," her mother said. "The host team never competes. It's against the rules. Spruce Hill is running things today. Their members will be on the course, spotting jumps and helping out if riders get lost."

She issued a raft of instructions.

"Holly and Robin, you unload the horses and get their bandages off. Jennifer and Sue, I want you to get our tack organized and ready to go." She turned toward Kate. "Run over to the secretary's booth and pick up course maps and our competitors' numbers." There was a pause. "And tell Angela to get over here and take care of her horse."

"What should I do?" Adam said.

"I think you'd better rejoin your team," Liz said, smiling. She reached up and ruffled his blond hair. "Go on, or they'll think you've defected to the enemy."

On her way to the secretary's booth, Kate passed a huge tent filled with tables and chairs. Catering staff in white coats bustled about, setting up warming trays and fussing with flower arrangements. Kate's stomach rumbled. All she'd had for breakfast was a dry bagel.

"Hey, wait up," Adam said, behind her.

She turned. "What's wrong?"

"Nothing." He grinned. "Except Holly's birthday."

It was coming up next month—something else Kate would miss because of Dad's new job. "I won't be here," she said, kicking at a clump of dirt.

Adam's face fell. "I was hoping you'd help me plan, like, a surprise party, or something. I've already cleared it with Liz."

"Text me," Kate said, "and I'll do what I can."

But it wouldn't be much. By the time Holly turned fifteen the weekend before Thanksgiving, Kate would be in Wyoming and Tapestry would be with her. She was going to make sure of that.

After Adam loped off, Kate collected her team's numbers from the secretary and grabbed a couple of maps. The hunter pace course was full of twists and turns, and some of the jumps had scary names like *the coffin* and *zombie ditch*. Kate was so engrossed in the map that she didn't notice Angela till the girl was almost on top of her.

As usual, she was dressed to kill—cream breeches, a well-tailored hunt jacket, and Ariat show boots. Her helmet was tucked beneath one arm; her black hair hung loose around her shoulders. Liz had told everyone to wear team sweatshirts, body protectors, and everyday breeches. Maybe Angela missed that message or, more than likely, ignored it.

"Give me that," Angela said.

She snatched the map from Kate's hands, gave it a cursory glance, and stuffed it in her pocket. Kate was about to object when Courtney and Derek Thompson strolled up. He shot a look at Kate, and she remembered where she'd seen him before. He'd won second place in her pleasure class at the Labor Day show. She'd been right behind him, in third.

"Oh, Derek," Angela said. "You'll take care of Courtney for me, won't you? She doesn't know anything about horses, and she needs an expert like you to help her out. I'll be too busy, riding with Kate."

Angela's syrupy voice made Kate's teeth ache.

She glanced at Derek Thompson, convinced he'd burst out laughing. But he was gazing at Angela's cousin like a cartoon character that's just been conked on the head with a frying pan. Courtney simpered and moved closer. She laid a hand on Derek's arm and batted her eyes, and Kate could swear he was about to pass out.

His face turned redder than Angela's fingernails.

"Tell me about your riding, Derek," Courtney gushed. "I want you to teach me everything you know." Tucking her arm through his, she led him away.

Angela smirked and gave a little sigh.

"Liz is looking for you," Kate said, fighting the urge to strangle her riding partner. "Your horse needs attention."

"Tell her I'll be along in a minute," Angela said.

Kate bit her lip.

This wasn't the time to pick a fight with Angela, not when she needed her cooperation to win the hunter pace and impress her father. He still hadn't called. She was about to head back to her teammates when Holly ran up.

Breathlessly, she said, "Kate, your father's here."

"Where?"

"Over by the van, talking to Mom."

But all Kate saw was a guy wearing chinos and an Australian bush hat. He was slender, with a beard and a tan. That wasn't her father. Dad was dumpy and clean shaven, and he never wore hats.

He turned toward her and smiled, then held out his arms.

* * *

It was like being hugged by a teddy bear. Dad's beard tickled her cheek. Kate felt warm and protected. Over to one side, she saw Liz smiling and nodding. Holly was grinning like someone who'd just gotten her braces off. For a moment or two, it was just the four of them—almost like a real family.

The announcer told everyone to get ready.

Dad pulled away. "Let's see this horse of yours."

Proudly, Kate introduced him to Tapestry. Her coat shone like a new penny, her mane and tail glistened, and she eagerly wuffled up the carrots Dad pulled from the pockets of his khaki vest. That was different, too. He always wore tweed jackets with leather patches on the elbows, not an outfit that smacked of Dora the Explorer.

He patted Tapestry's nose. "She's prettier than *Lycaena phlaeas*."

Liz said, "I take it that's high praise?"

"You bet," Kate said. "It's his favorite butterfly." She ran a hand over Tapestry's sparkly browband, a gift from Holly to celebrate Tapestry's arrival at the barn.

"Cute," said her father. "Makes her look like a princess."

"That's because she is," Kate said.

Things were looking good. Dad was smiling and enjoying himself. But best of all, he was admiring her horse. Kate remembered the exhibitor numbers she was holding and gave them to Liz. She handed them out; Kate and Angela were pair number thirteen.

Thirteen?

Kate gulped. She liked to think she wasn't superstitious, but any number other than thirteen would've been a whole lot better. She tied the number to her body protector, slipped into it, and watched Holly and Jennifer ride toward the starting gate. They were followed by Adam and Kristina James.

In ten minutes it would be her turn.

Angela pinned her number to Skywalker's saddle pad. She wasn't wearing a body protector, unless it was hidden beneath her hunt jacket. But Kate doubted it. She looked too sleek and slender.

"Is that your partner?" Dad said.

"Yes."

"She's a pretty girl," he said. "Are you good friends?"

"Not exactly," Kate said, as she tightened Tapestry's girth. She glanced at Angela, now mounted on Skywalker and fiddling with her cell phone.

"You don't have time for texting," Liz said. "You and Kate need to get ready."

Angela looked up and for a split second, Kate saw a guilty look flash across her partner's face. Angela shoved the phone in her pocket and rode off to join Courtney, still fawning over Derek.

Kate stuck her foot in the stirrup and settled herself

into the saddle. She pulled on her brown leather gloves and made sure her helmet was fastened securely.

"Good luck," her father said. He patted Tapestry's neck and leaned close enough to whisper in her ear. "You take good care of my daughter. Don't you dare come back without her."

Tapestry whickered and gave a little nod.

"She understands you," Kate said.

"She'd better," her father said. "I'm counting on her."

Dad's enthusiasm was encouraging. He'd never shown much interest in her riding before. Maybe Tapestry was having some sort of magical effect on him, or maybe Vermont was. Perhaps if she tried hard enough, she could persuade him that they really did need to live here. But they couldn't live here unless Dad had a job, and butterfly professors weren't exactly in high demand.

Unless …

No, that was totally out of the question.

Her father would never consider working at a butterfly museum. Kate shoved Holly's crazy idea firmly out of her mind and trotted toward Angela and Courtney. Derek had disappeared. As she got closer, Kate heard snatches of whispered conversation. The words *stupid* and *boys are so dumb* floated toward her.

"Are you ready?" she said to Angela.

"More than you'll ever be," Angela retorted. She dug her heels into Skywalker's sides and cantered off.

"Angela knows how to ride the course," Courtney said. "So you'd better listen up." With a dismissive sniff, she turned away.

Kate stared after her. What on earth was Courtney talking about? She didn't know the first thing about horses, and Angela didn't have a clue how to ride a hunter pace. She hadn't come to one single practice session.

"Five minutes," Liz signaled.

Gathering up her reins, Kate trotted and cantered a few circles, then jogged over to join Angela. The starting gate was a pair of white jump stands. Two men with stopwatches stood on either side. One of them had a whistle around his neck; the other wore a Batman mask.

Tapestry wasn't too keen about standing beside Angela's fractious horse. Skywalker pinned his ears, and Tapestry skittered sideways like a crab.

"You'd better keep up with me," Angela said. She wore spurs and carried a stiff crop.

Urgently, Kate said, "It's not a race. It's a—"

But the starter's whistle drowned out her words.

4

ANGELA WHACKED SKYWALKER with her crop, and they surged through the gate like a tidal wave. For a few strides, Kate and Tapestry matched them, but Angela and her horse raced ahead. Within minutes, they were over the first jump and galloping for the next. Kate caught up with them as the course veered into the woods. Orange ribbons tied to tree trunks marked the way.

"Slow down," Kate said. "This is much too fast."

"I know what I'm doing," Angela snapped. She wheeled Skywalker around and tore off, leaving Kate no choice but to scramble along behind.

The next fence was a line of truck tires, with a teepee of branches at each end. On top of one sat a scarecrow, legs stuffed with hay and wearing a tattered straw hat.

Skywalker skidded to a halt. Angela gave him another whack, but he lurched to one side and almost unseated her. She hauled herself back in the saddle and fumbled for her stirrups.

"I'll jump it," Kate yelled. One of them had to.

Tightening her grip, she aimed Tapestry at the tires. It looked kind of scary, but her mare didn't even hesitate. She cleared the rubber jump with plenty of room to spare.

"Hurry up," Angela said, circling her impatient horse.

The trail spilled into a large, sloping meadow. Ahead lay two more jumps. The coffin was a long black box open at one end with a fake body inside; the other jump was the zombie ditch filled with pumpkins. Angela raked Skywalker with her spurs and he flew over both obstacles, so Kate rode around them. They'd be finished with this course way too soon if Angela didn't slow down.

But all of a sudden, she did, and by the time Kate cantered up, Angela was frowning at her iPhone. Skywalker, breathing hard, kept dancing sideways. Angela jerked his reins.

Kate said, "You're not gonna text are you?"

"Don't be an idiot." Angela shoved the phone in her pocket. "We're going too fast."

"Duh-uh," Kate said. "That's what I've been trying to tell you."

"We'll do a slow canter for the next part," Angela said. "Then we'll trot again afterward, when we reach the woods."

It was like she'd actually studied the course, but Kate knew she hadn't. Angela never studied anything. She relied on luck and cheating to get her through whatever needed getting through.

"So, who died and left you in charge?" Kate said.

Angela glared at her. "I want to win, and I know you do because you need to impress your father with Tapestry so he won't force you to sell her."

Kate gasped. How had Angela figured that one out?

"And I know how to win and you don't," Angela said. "So just shut up and follow me and we'll both get what we want."

Without another word, she made for a gap in the stone wall. On the other side was an old cornfield; beyond it lay more trees. Angela kept up a steady pace. She cantered between the stubbly furrows, jumped a set of rustic poles, then looped around a farm wagon. Orange signs blazed a trail back into the woods. Angela stopped in a clearing and pulled out her iPhone.

"It's time to trot now," she said.

Feeling uneasy, Kate followed. Angela was acting as if she actually knew how long it had taken the pacesetter to ride the course. But that was ridiculous. Nobody knew except the officials. Angela was doing this just to freak her out.

Kate pushed her doubts to one side. She jumped a fallen tree, popped over another ditch, and waved to the spotters at both jumps. The trail widened and curved to the right. Once they were far enough away from the spotters, Angela stopped again. Out came her phone.

"We've got five minutes left," she muttered more to herself than to Kate.

Kate stared at her. "How do you know?"

"Because I can tell time," Angela snapped. "And because I know how to count, okay? I'm not completely stupid."

Kate swallowed her anger. Arguing was hopeless, and she couldn't finish the hunter pace without her partner. All she could do was wait until Princess Angela decided it was time for them to get going again.

* * *

Angela's sister and her cousin were waiting as they rode across the finish line. Kate could hear Holly cheering.

"How did it go?" Courtney said. She tossed her mane of blond hair over one shoulder.

"Fine," Angela said. "But no thanks to Kate."

"Didn't she—?"

Angela held up her hand. "I'll tell you later."

With a contemptuous look at Kate, Angela jumped off her sweaty horse and tossed his reins to Marcia. Then she linked arms with her cousin and they sauntered toward the food tent. Marcia released Skywalker's girth, ran up the stirrups, and led her sister's horse away. His head drooped; his sides heaved. He looked even more exhausted than Kate felt.

But it wasn't physical exhaustion; it was the mental stress of dealing with Angela that wiped Kate out. She slid off her horse and her legs buckled. Breathing hard, she loosened Tapestry's girth.

Holly ran up with a cooler. "You'll never guess who's here," she said, draping the green blanket over Tapestry's back.

Kate was too tired to play games. "Who?"

"The Gorgon."

For a moment, it didn't register. "Mrs. Gordon?"

"Yeah," Holly said. "Our high school principal has cornered your father in the food tent and they're yapping about butterflies."

41

"Oops," Kate said. "I forgot to ask him about giving that talk."

"The Gorgon's probably doing it for you," Holly said, grinning. "I bet they're BBFFs by now."

"BBFF?"

"Butterfly best friends forever." Holly flapped a pair of imaginary wings and took Tapestry's reins from Kate. "What did you think of the course? Wasn't it awesome?"

"Yeah," Kate said, trying to sound enthusiastic.

"Magician jumped everything," Holly said. "Even those horrible tires. Rebel wouldn't go anywhere near them. Poor Jennifer. I thought he was going to buck her off." She paused to catch her breath. "Robin and Sue got lost, and Adam said Kristina's horse refused the coffin so he had to jump it, but Domino had a fit over the zombie ditch, and ..."

As Holly chattered on, Kate couldn't get her mind off Angela's iPhone. There was something about it that disturbed her. But what? Slowly, she removed her helmet and ran a hand through her sticky wet hair. "I'm a mess."

"Yup," Holly said. "Look, I'll cool Tapestry off and put her in the van. You can hit the restroom and fix yourself up."

"Thanks," Kate said. "Where is it?"

"In the barn." Holly dug into her pocket and pulled out a small hairbrush. "Take this, too."

* * *

The Spruce Hill restroom was positively luxurious compared to the cramped little toilet at Timber Ridge. It had two stalls, a sink with taps that actually worked, and a tiny mirror. Kate dragged Holly's brush through her hair, wiped her face, and was about to leave when she heard familiar voices.

Quickly, she hid inside the end stall.

"I bet Kate was surprised when you made her slow down," came Courtney's voice.

"Yeah," said Angela. "I thought she was going to argue when we stopped in the woods, right before the finish. But I don't think she suspects anything."

She gave a nasty laugh that turned Kate's knees to jelly. She leaned against the stall's partition and hoped they wouldn't look beneath it and see her boots.

"Thanks for getting the time," Angela said. "I owe you one."

There was the sound of running water, and Courtney's reply was fragmented. "It was easy ... dumb kid ... batted my eyes, and ..."

The water stopped. "I bet he melted when you told

him how cute he looked in his riding breeches," Angela said.

"Like butter in the sun," Courtney replied. "Then he couldn't wait to tell me that *he* was the one who'd set the pace." She giggled. "I promised not to tell, but he made me swear on his great-grandmother's grave."

"Ugh," Angela said. "Is she buried in the paddock?"

"I think she's a witch on the barn's roof."

Angela laughed. "There's no way I can lose now," she said, sounding confident. "I kept checking the time, and I think we came within ten or fifteen seconds."

Kate almost cried out. She clamped a hand over her mouth and froze in place. If they hung about much longer, she'd explode and—

The outer door clanged shut. For a moment, Kate didn't dare move. Suppose they came back? Suppose one of them decided she had to use the toilet after all?

After what felt like an hour but was probably only a minute, Kate opened the stall door and crept out. She washed her hands and wished she could wash out her ears as well. Angela *had* found a way to cheat, and she'd dragged Kate into it as well.

Kate yanked off her number.

Thirteen.

She dumped it in the trash, then trudged toward the food tent battling with her conscience. Half of her wanted to come clean; the other half told her to wait and see if they were beaten. If they were, she didn't need to say a word about Angela's cheating. But if they won a ribbon, Kate would have to spill the beans.

She wouldn't be able to live with herself if she didn't.

* * *

Kate grabbed a plate and stared at the buffet table, but her appetite had vanished. She felt queasy just looking at the platters of glazed ham, home fries, quiches, and smoked salmon. But she had to eat something. She settled for yogurt and a blueberry muffin.

There was a punch bowl filled with hot cider and cinnamon sticks. A jug beside it held something pink and frothy. Kate felt her stomach churn. The last pair had already finished the course, but the results wouldn't be announced until everyone had eaten.

"Over here," Kate's dad called out.

Swallowing the urge to bolt, Kate made her way toward him. She dodged waiters, squeezed between tables, and narrowly missed tripping over a small terrier that had wound its leash around several chair legs.

"How was your ride?" her father said.

She shrugged. "It was fine, I guess."

"Angela's been boasting that you guys are gonna win," Holly said, tucking into a mountain of fluffy scrambled eggs. She speared herself a sausage from Adam's plate.

"Hey, get your own," he complained.

"Kate, are you all right?" Liz said. "You look kind of pale."

Kate forced a smile. "I'm okay."

Liz seemed about to press further when the others showed up. Kate shifted over to make room for her teammates. Robin set down a stack of pancakes drowning in maple syrup, Sue nibbled on a peanut butter cookie the size of a Frisbee, and Jennifer's plate overflowed with strawberries and whipped cream.

"You guys are on a sugar high," Holly teased.

"We've earned it," Sue retorted.

They all started talking at once, but Kate tuned them out. Her father was trying to tell her about Mrs. Gordon and how she'd persuaded him to visit the high school before they moved to Wyoming.

"She's a forceful woman," he said. "Knows her butterflies, too."

"Did she leave?" Kate pushed away her half-eaten yogurt. Maybe the muffin would be better. She took a small bite, but it tasted like sawdust.

Her father nodded. "It's her turn to volunteer at the butterfly museum. She's invited me to stop by later on," he said with a wry grin.

Kate couldn't tell if her dad was pleased about this or was just making fun. So much about him had changed—his clothes, the beard, his new shape. He'd lost a lot of weight in the jungle.

The loudspeaker hummed into life.

"Ladies and gentlemen," said the announcer. "We have the final results."

Someone cheered, and Kate's tension rose. She glanced at her riding partner, who was sitting with Mrs. Dean and the Thompsons. Briefly, Angela caught her eye, then shrugged as if she didn't have a care in the world.

"In sixth place we have ..."

The announcer rattled off names faster than Kate could keep track of. Her heart was beating so hard that she was afraid to open her mouth in case it jumped out.

"... Jennifer West and Holly Chapman, from Timber Ridge ..."

Holly squealed with delight and for a split second Kate thought her best friend and Jennifer had won first place. Her relief soared like a kite ... but no, they'd come in third.

"Our second place winners are Adam Randolph and Kristina James, from Larchwood Equestrian Center," the announcer went on.

Adam pumped the air with both fists. His riding

partner appeared out of nowhere and kissed his cheek. Holly glared at her. Beneath the table, Kate crossed her fingers. She couldn't remember ever wanting to lose before.

The announcer cleared his throat. "And now for the winners," he said. "But before we get to that—" There was a dramatic pause, and Mrs. Dean's petulant voice broke the silence.

"Oh, come on, hurry up. Don't keep us waiting."

"We've had something of a record here today," the announcer said, shooting Angela's mother a frosty look. "Never before in the history of our hunter pace has a pair of riders come so close to the correct time."

Conversations halted. People stopped eating and an expectant hush settled over the crowd. Kate wanted to curl up and die. She knew exactly what was coming next.

"The winning pair, with a time only twelve seconds off the mark, is from Timber Ridge. Please congratulate Angela Dean and Kate McGregor," the announcer said. "Let's give these talented riders a round of applause."

"Well done," Liz shouted above the cheers.

Holly whooped, Sue hollered, and Jennifer gave Kate a high five. Robin said, "I knew you could do it."

"Fabulous job, Kate," her father said. He scooped her into another bear hug.

She pulled herself free. "I'm sorry."

"What's wrong?" His gray eyes were full of concern.

Kate turned toward Liz. "I've got to talk to you. Right now."

Liz's smile faded. "You don't look like someone who's just won a blue ribbon."

"That's the problem," Kate whispered. "I haven't."

She tugged at Liz's arm and led her to the back of the tent where nobody could hear them. She didn't want to explain Angela's miraculous ride over the hunter pace course in front of the others.

"Okay, what's all the mystery?" Liz said.

"Angela cheated."

"That's impossible," Liz said. "You can't cheat on a hunter pace."

5

KATE SHOOK HER HEAD. "Courtney flirted with Derek Thompson and persuaded him to tell her the correct time. She told Angela just before we set off, and—"

"Angela kept track of it on her iPhone?" Liz said.

Miserably, Kate nodded. "It's got a stopwatch app."

"How did you find out?"

"I heard them bragging about it when I was in the bathroom," Kate said. "They didn't know I was there, and—"

"I'm proud of you," Liz said, with a catch in her voice. "You could've kept quiet about this and nobody would have known."

There was an awkward silence, and Kate felt herself blushing. She was innocent, so why did she feel guilty?

"Liz, you don't think I had anything to do with it, do you?"

"Of course not," Liz said.

"So, what should I do?"

"Nothing," Liz said. "I'll take care of it." She guided Kate toward the tent's rear flap. "Go to the van and hug your horse. I'll send Holly out to keep you company."

"What about my dad?"

Liz raised an eyebrow. "That's up to you."

"I'll tell him myself later," Kate said, dreading it. Dad would have a hard time understanding this one. In his gentle world, anything as pretty as Angela had gossamer wings—not fangs and sharp claws.

* * *

Inside the van, Kate wrapped her arms around Tapestry's warm neck. Everything had turned out wrong, and it was Angela's fault. Kate didn't want to give in to her tears, but they came anyway. Tapestry whickered, and Kate hugged her even harder.

She was still crying when Holly ran up the ramp.

"What's wrong? Mom's in a big huddle with the judges. They've held back our ribbons, and Mrs. Dean's about to have a meltdown."

Kate wiped her nose with her sleeve. It was obvious

from Holly's expression that Liz hadn't told her what happened. Between sobs, Kate gasped out the details.

"Cripes," Holly said. "I was only kidding when I said Angela would figure out a way to cheat. She's smarter than I thought."

"I wish I hadn't entered the stupid hunter pace," Kate said. "I feel awful."

"You'll feel even worse when Angela finds out you've squealed on her," Holly said.

"Thanks a lot," Kate said. "That's a real help."

"I'm sorry, but it's true. She'll be all over you for this," Holly said. "You'd better keep out of her way or wear a flak vest around the barn."

Kate smiled through her tears. She could always rely on Holly to make her laugh, no matter how miserable she felt. "Well, at least you can thank me."

"What for?"

"You dummy," Kate said, sniffing. "You and Jennifer are in second place now."

"Wow," Holly said. "I hadn't thought of that."

Kate said, "Which means Adam's won the blue ribbon."

"So has Kristina," Holly muttered. "I'll smack her if she kisses him again."

There was a gentle tap on the van. "Kate, are you all right?"

"It's Dad," Kate whispered. "I've got to tell him, but I don't know where to begin. I mean, how do you explain someone like Angela? He doesn't understand kids. He'll think I'm making it up, or—"

"He won't," Holly said. "Your dad's kind of cool. He told me he didn't like cutting up his first frog either."

* * *

Kate had never thought of her father as cool before, but Holly was right. Within minutes, he got the big picture and wrapped Kate in yet another hug, saying the same as Liz about being proud of her for telling the truth.

"Angela's going to kill me," Kate moaned.

"Over my dead body," he said.

It made Kate smile.

"See?" Holly said, nudging her. "What did I tell you?"

Liz ran up and told Holly the ribbons would be given out in five minutes. She patted Kate's arm. "It's all settled. You can stay out here if you want, or—"

"What did you tell the judges?" Kate said.

She cringed at the thought of Liz explaining how pair number thirteen had gamed the system. Even though Kate hadn't done anything wrong, her name was tied to Angela's. The judges probably thought both of them had cheated.

Gently, Liz said, "I just told them you'd withdrawn."

"That's all?" Kate said. "Didn't they think that was kind of weird?"

"Only for a few seconds," Liz said. "They were too busy rectifying the results to argue with me."

"What about Angela?" Kate said.

Holly chimed in. "Yeah, Mom. What did you say to *her*?"

"Just that I knew she'd cheated and that I'd pulled her and Kate from the competition," Liz said, running a hand through her untidy hair. "I also told her that I was angry and disappointed and that if she ever pulled something like this again, she was off the riding team."

"Where is she now?" Holly said.

"Last I saw, Mrs. Dean was demanding they go home," Liz said. "I certainly would if I were in their shoes."

"Does Angela know it was me who ratted on her?" Kate said, trying to suppress a shudder. Even though she'd done the right thing, it didn't sit well on her shoulders. She hated being a whistle blower.

"I kept your name out of it," Liz said. "So how could she?"

"Come on, Mom," Holly said. "Angela's not stupid."

Liz sighed. "It'll be over and forgotten in a few days."

"Don't count on it," Holly said. "I bet Angela's already put a curse on Kate." She shot her best friend an evil grin. "I promise not to cut you up if Angela turns you into a frog."

Despite herself, Kate laughed.

Just then, the loudspeaker reminded everyone that the awards ceremony was about to begin, but Kate decided not to go. She didn't dare risk running into Angela and Courtney. It would be just like them to hide in the shadows, ready to pounce on her.

* * *

Kate's father cheered louder than she did when Holly, Jennifer, and Adam emerged from the food tent, waving their ribbons and grinning broadly. Kristina James tried to muscle in, but Holly elbowed her out of the way.

After Kate gave Holly a high five, Sue and Robin clapped Jennifer on the back so hard she almost fell over. Ben McGregor congratulated all the riders and then asked Kate if she'd drive back to the barn with him.

"But first, I'd like to stop at the museum," he said.

Kate was torn. She wanted to go with her friends so they could celebrate, but being with Dad was super important. It might be their only chance to be alone together. He'd be staying with Aunt Marion in the village tonight and then driving back to Connecticut tomorrow.

On Tuesday, he was flying out to Wyoming and expected Kate to join him the following weekend. She wasn't much good at explaining how she felt about this, but she had to try. Doing it in the car, with Dad as a captive audience, was the best shot she had.

"Go," Liz said. "We'll take care of your horse."

"And Skywalker," Holly said. "Princess Angela has finked out again."

Good thing, too, Kate thought as she slipped into the van. The last thing she wanted was to face Angela. Kate gave Tapestry a kiss and a carrot, then followed her father to his rental car.

As they pulled out of the parking lot, Kate inhaled the magnificent view. With its red barn and rolling meadows, Spruce Hill Farm looked like a travel poster for Vermont. In the distance, a white church steeple poked up among the trees. Beyond were the mountains of Killington Ski Resort. Several peaks had snow on top.

"There'll be good skiing in Wyoming," her father said.

"There's good skiing here," Kate said, wondering why they were talking about winter sports. Neither of them knew how to ski. She'd never learned, and her father had two left feet when it came to anything athletic.

He glanced at her. "You really love it here, don't you?"

"Yes," Kate said. "Holly's the best friend I've ever had, and Liz is a great riding instructor, and—" She choked up. "I don't want to live in Wyoming if it means leaving my horse behind."

There. It was out.

For a moment, her father was quiet. Then he said, "Kate, I'm sorry about this, but I don't have much choice. I have to go where—"

"Can't I stay here?" Kate blurted, close to tears.

"With the Chapmans?" he said.

"Yes."

"Have they invited you?"

"Yes ... no," Kate said. "Well, not exactly. But they will. Holly wants me to move in with them. So, please ... *can* I?"

Kate knew she was acting like a spoiled brat. She sounded worse than Marcia Dean pleading for a horse of her own. But she couldn't help it. Just once, she wanted to stamp her foot and get her own way.

All her life she'd been sensible, the good girl who followed the rules and never caused a fuss. She'd never complained about her father tramping through jungles from Borneo to Brazil while she was shunted off to various relatives. This summer had been Aunt Marion's turn, but it only lasted a week because Kate had found a job at Timber Ridge and moved in with Holly and Liz.

"No," her father said gently. "You're all I've got"—he caught his breath—"and I love you."

Kate gulped. He'd never said that before, not even when her mom was alive. She knew Dad loved her, but it was a little unnerving to actually hear him say it.

"You're never around," she said, sounding petulant even to her own ears. "You're always off somewhere, chasing dumb butterflies."

"Not any more." He yanked the steering wheel to avoid an oncoming tractor. The farmer driving it shook his fist as they shot past. Kate's heart got stuck in her throat. Dad's driving had always alarmed her.

He said, "My research is finished, so I'll be writing my next book, along with teaching a few courses." He patted her knee. "We'll have a great new life in Wyoming, just you wait and see."

But Kate didn't want to.

Somehow, she had to find a rock-solid reason for them both to stay in Vermont. Two rock-solid reasons would be even better.

* * *

The butterfly museum was called "Dancing Wings." It had a big sign out front showing a Monarch butterfly wearing ballet slippers and a pink tutu. Inwardly, Kate groaned. Dad was going to hate this. *Hate* it.

Oddly enough, he didn't.

Mrs. Gordon swooped out from behind the welcome desk and gave them a guided tour. The conservatory was much bigger than Kate had expected. Butterflies and moths fluttered gracefully among tropical plants, Japanese koi swam lazily in tranquil ponds, and Dad was utterly charmed when a Leopard Lacewing landed on his arm and refused to get off. He winked at Kate and acted like a kid who'd never seen a butterfly up close before.

"We have more than four thousand native and tropical butterflies here," said Mrs. Gordon, sounding proud. "And we attract visitors from all over"—she glanced at Kate—"including grad students and Doctor Rueben Zimmerman."

He was Dad's old professor and arch rival. He'd written more butterfly books and articles than her father had.

"Impressive," he said, nodding. "Tell me about your academic programs and science fairs."

"I'd be glad to," Mrs. Gordon said.

Kate watched, openmouthed, as her high school principal linked arms with her father and led him through a door marked *Private—Staff Only*. Did Mrs. Gordon have a weird sixth sense about this? Did she know how much Kate wanted to stay in Vermont and was doing her best to make it happen?

Holly was absolutely *not* going to believe this one.

Twenty minutes later it got even weirder.

While her dad was skimming books in the gift shop, Mrs. Gordon slipped Kate a brochure about the butterfly museum. On it she'd written, *It's for sale.*

* * *

Holly's face took on its *I told you so* expression when Kate explained her plan. They were in the barn settling their horses down for the night. Dad and Liz were at the house making dinner, which probably meant charred hot dogs or mac and cheese from a box, given that neither of them knew much about cooking. With luck, they'd give up and send out for pizza.

"I want Dad to buy the butterfly museum," Kate said, gazing at Tapestry over her stall door. After all they'd been through, Kate still couldn't quite believe that Tapestry belonged to her.

Holly rolled her eyes. "*Told* you."

"But he's got to think it's his idea, not mine," Kate said.

"Does he have enough money?"

"I don't know," Kate said. "That's the problem. I bet it's really expensive, and Dad probably doesn't have anything saved up."

"If you move here, you'll have to sell your condo,"

Holly said. "He could use that money to buy the museum."

"Then where would we live?" Kate said.

"With the butterflies?"

Kate sighed. Her brilliant idea was starting to unravel. It had all seemed so simple ten minutes ago, before she'd actually put it into words by telling Holly. "What else can we do?"

"You said we need two big reasons to get your dad to stay here," Holly said, frowning. "The museum is one, but we have to think of another."

"Like what?"

Holly's cell phone chirped. "Yeah, Mom, we're almost done. We'll be home in five, okay?" She hung up and pinned Kate with a look. "How about a girlfriend?"

Kate almost choked. "My father? You're dreaming."

"No, I'm dead serious," Holly said. "Unless you've got a better idea."

6

ON THEIR WAY BACK TO THE HOUSE, Holly regaled Kate with details of old musicals. The other night she'd watched reruns of *Mary Poppins* and *The Sound of Music*. Both movies starred kids who trumped the clueless grownups. But her favorite was a Disney film called *The Parent Trap*.

"It's about two girls," Holly said. "Twins. They were separated when they were babies 'cause their parents got divorced. One girl was raised by her mother, the other by her dad, and they didn't even know about each other till they accidentally met at summer camp, and—"

"We're not twins, we're not even sisters," Kate said, wishing they were. "And our parents weren't married to each other." She scuffed her feet through furrows of dry mud. "They only met this morning."

"Pfffft," Holly said, as if it were a mere detail. "The point is, the girls got their parents back together again."

"Fantasy," Kate said. "A Hollywood fairy tale."

"And it could be ours," Holly said.

She shot Kate a knowing look and stomped through the back door. The welcome smell of pepperoni pizza wafted out.

* * *

Kate's father was still wearing his trendy outfit, but Liz had changed into a denim skirt, high-heeled boots, and a cable-knit sweater that matched her blue eyes. She'd even put on lip gloss and scooped her honey blond hair into one of Holly's scrunchies. Kate couldn't remember ever seeing Liz in a skirt before. There were candles on the kitchen table, a bottle of red wine, and real cloth napkins.

"Fancy," Holly said. "Even the dishes match."

They demolished both pizzas and were about to tuck into bowls of buttercrunch ice cream when Liz said, "Kate, your dad and I have been talking."

Holly gave Kate a sharp nudge under the table.

"About Tapestry," Liz went on. "We've come up with an idea that I think you'll like."

"I get to keep her?"

"Not exactly," her father said, dragging out each syllable as if it were painful. He glanced at Liz.

She smiled. "I'd like to buy her."

For a moment, Kate sat in stunned silence. Tapestry was a registered Morgan. Her original owner had said she was worth at least five thousand dollars. Liz didn't have that kind money, and even if she did, Kate didn't want to sell Tapestry—not even to Liz.

Fighting back tears, she said, "My horse isn't for sale."

"Be reasonable, Kate," her father said. He reached for her hand but she snatched it away. "We'll get you a fine new horse in Wyoming, I promise."

"I don't want a new horse. I want Tapestry," Kate said.

Holly gave her another nudge and stood up. She'd already devoured her ice cream. "I've got a ton of homework and I need Kate's help."

Kate opened her mouth to argue but shut it again. Neither of them had homework. They'd done it all the night before. While her father and Liz exchanged odd looks the way parents do when their kids aren't playing by the rules, Kate scuttled off to join Holly in their shared bedroom.

"What's wrong?" Kate said. "You don't really have more homework, do you?"

"No, I need you to shut up."

"Huh?" With difficulty, Kate folded herself onto

Holly's old wooden rocking horse. It creaked beneath her.

"Stop arguing," Holly said. "Let Mom and your dad think you're okay about selling Tapestry ... for now."

"Why?"

"So we can put the real plan into action." Holly struck a pose and put both hands on her hips. "Look, I know you think that old movie is stupid, but it's a place to start. We just need to get our parents together, without us hanging about."

"Like a blind date?"

"Yes," Holly said. "But it's kind of hard when Mom lives here and your dad's in Connecticut."

"Or Wyoming," Kate said, miserably.

"Which means we've got to work fast," Holly said.

"Okay," Kate said. "So what's the plan?"

She could almost hear the wheels in Holly's brain turning. Once her best friend latched onto an idea, she refused to let go. Holly was like a kitten with a ball of yarn. The trouble was, things tended to get all tangled up rather than sorted out.

"How about we buy them tickets for the same cruise?" Holly said. "They'd be stuck on a boat for three days and they'd have to hang out together."

"Brilliant," Kate said. "There's just one problem."

"What?" Holly said.

The wooden rocking horse let out another creak as Kate climbed off it. She grabbed her piggy bank and shook it. "Who's gonna pay for it?"

Holly frowned. "Okay, then how about tickets for a show? Our parents would be sitting next to each another in a dark theater, and—"

"—they'd smell a rat," Kate said.

With a dramatic sigh, Holly collapsed onto her unmade bed. "There's got to be *something* we can do."

"There is," Kate said. "We just haven't thought of it yet."

Getting her father together with Liz was something Kate had often dreamed about, but that's all it was—a dream. Ever since her mom died five years ago, her dad had never looked at another woman, let alone dated one. The only thing that would keep him in Vermont was the perfect job.

Kate picked up the butterfly museum brochure and looked at Mrs. Gordon's note. Had she told Dad the museum was for sale, or was she relying on Kate to mention it? He hadn't said a word, so maybe—

"I've got it," Holly shrieked, sitting bolt upright. "We'll run away like Hansel and Gretel. Our parents will be so upset that they'll get together to come and find us."

Kate folded the brochure and threw it at her like a

paper dart. "You watch too many dumb movies," she said. "If we run off, they'll call the police, and we'll be grounded for six months."

There was a soft tap on the door. "Girls," Liz said. "Kate's dad is about to leave."

"He's gonna be mad at me," Kate whispered.

"Nah," Holly said. "Just don't talk about Tapestry, okay? Tell him you can't wait to see Wyoming."

"Yeah, right," Kate said, pulling a face. "He'll see through that in a nanosecond."

"He won't," Holly said. "Trust me. It's what he wants to hear, so he'll believe you. Now, stop scowling. Pretend like you're okay with everything."

Forcing a smile, Kate watched the bedroom door swing open. There stood her father, looking sad-eyed like a puppy that's just been scolded for chewing up a slipper. For a second or two, neither of them moved, then he pulled Kate into an awkward hug. She felt herself stiffen. Inside, she was a mess of guilt and anxiety, and the pizza she'd just eaten was threatening to stage a comeback.

Her father said, "I've cleared it with Mrs. Gordon for you to take Friday off school. Aunt Marion will drive you to the airport, and I'll be waiting for you in Laramie."

Wyoming.

The other side of the earth.

Well, not exactly, but it felt that way to Kate. "Okay," she said, swallowing hard.

Behind her, Holly let out a sigh.

* * *

After school on Tuesday, Kate paid a long overdue visit to Aunt Marion in the village. Her cottage was surrounded by roses. They climbed over the front door, jostled for attention along the front path, and covered every inch of her tiny back yard. Even now, in late October, several roses were still in full bloom.

"You don't want to leave, do you?" Aunt Marion said. She snipped off two broken stems and dropped her pruning shears into a plastic bucket.

"No," Kate said, "but Dad says we've got to." She caught her breath. "And he says I've got to sell Tapestry, too."

"Can't you get another horse in Wyoming?"

Kate shook her head. Aunt Marion meant well, but she didn't know any more about horses than Dad did. "I want Dad to stay here and buy the butterfly museum. It's for sale, and—"

"My brother, the bug expert, in charge of a tourist trap?" Aunt Marion said, stripping off her leather gloves. "It sounds like a lepidopterist's nightmare."

"Not this one," Kate said. "Even Dad's old professor approves of it." She followed her aunt into the cottage's tiny kitchen. There were boxes piled everywhere. Persy, Aunt Marion's black kitten, sat washing his paws on top of a laundry basket full of gardening books.

"Sorry about the mess," Aunt Marion said.

Astonished, Kate looked around. "Are you moving, too?"

"Just for the winter," her aunt said, pouring Kate a glass of milk. "I've rented a house in South Carolina. If it works out, I might move permanently. It all depends on whether I really can grow bigger roses down there like people tell me."

"When are you leaving?" Kate said.

"In a couple of weeks," Aunt Marion said. "Now, about Friday morning. Your father says I'm to pick you up at six o'clock." She faked a yawn, then pulled a pack of Oreos from the cupboard and offered them to Kate. "Does he know about your crazy plan?"

"Not yet," Kate said, twisting her cookie apart and eating the creamy inside. "But it's a really cool idea."

"Why?" said her aunt.

Kate chose her words carefully. "My high school principal volunteers there. She says a lot of scientists use the butterfly museum for research and they have graduate students to help out, plus it would be a great place for Dad to sell his books and he'd have time to write more, but—"

"You'd like me to help?" Aunt Marion said.

"Yes," Kate said, grateful her aunt had figured out the problem immediately. "Dad will listen to you."

"That would be a first," Aunt Marion said. "I'm fifteen years older than your father, but he's never paid a lick of attention to my advice."

"Oh," Kate said, swallowing her disappointment.

Her aunt scooped up the kitten and parked herself in a chair across from Kate. "Here's the deal," she said, stroking Persy's shiny black fur. "If you can convince my stubborn brother that this butterfly caper is a good idea, you can live in my cottage for the winter, rent-free."

"Wow," Kate said. "Is this for real?"

"Absolutely," said Aunt Marion. "Just promise not to ride your horse over my rose bushes, okay?"

* * *

Feeling encouraged, Kate took a late bus up to the barn. Holly and the others were at Sue's house making costumes for Halloween. They would all be witches riding broomsticks, except none of them could figure out how to turn their horses into brooms.

Sue said they should make corn brooms and tie lengthwise to their horses' saddles. Jennifer suggested they paint the brooms on. Robin, always the voice of reason, pointed out that people wouldn't even notice the brooms. They'd be so thrilled to see horses on their front doorsteps, they'd be racing back into their kitchens for apples and carrots.

The sour taste of envy bubbled up in Kate's throat.

She never used to like Halloween parties, but this one sounded like more fun than enough, and she really wanted to go. To take her mind off it, she brushed Tapestry more vigorously than usual. Dust and horse hair clung to her green hoodie; her new jeans were smeared with mud. She should've changed clothes at the house before bringing Tapestry in from the paddock.

Behind her a small voice said, "Can I give Tapestry a carrot?"

Kate whipped around and saw Marcia Dean peering over the stall door. Angela's ten-year-old sister was so short, only her freckled nose and brown eyes were visible. Frizzy red curls stuck out from beneath her helmet. She looked nothing like her older sister or her mother. They had pale blue eyes and hair the color of coal.

"Sure," Kate said. "She'd love it."

Marcia opened the stall door and slipped inside. Tapestry whickered when she saw Marcia's carrot. She stretched out her nose and whuffled it up, then looked for more.

"Greedy girl," Marcia said, patting Kate's mare. She gave a wistful sigh. "Tapestry's such a pretty horse. I wish I had one exactly like her."

Kate opened her mouth, then shut it again. No matter what she said, it would sound patronizing. Marcia was a decent little rider, and she'd already outgrown the barn's beginner ponies. In a few years, she'd be a much better horsewoman than Angela was. Nicer, too.

"Would you like to ride Tapestry?" Kate said, surprising herself. She hadn't meant to offer. The words just slipped out.

Marcia's eyes grew as big as saucers. "Like, right now?"

"Why not?" Kate said, warming to the idea. "You've got your helmet on, so let's go."

"YOU ACTUALLY LET HER ride Tapestry?" Holly said. She slammed her math book on the kitchen table. "Are you nuts? She's Angela's sister, remember? She's, like, the *enemy*?"

"C'mon, Holly," Kate said. "Marcia's a nice little kid who was born into the wrong family. All we did was walk around the arena, and then I lunged her at a slow trot."

"Did you clear it with Mom?"

"Of course, I did," Kate snapped. "I'm not totally stupid."

Holly gasped, and Kate realized with a shock that she sounded just like Angela on the hunter pace course. "I'm sorry," she said. "I'm kind of—"

"Stressed out?" Holly said.

Miserably, Kate nodded. Her life was a hot mess, and Liz hadn't helped. After giving Kate the go-ahead with Marcia, she'd added—almost as an afterthought—that Tapestry would make a great horse for Angela's little sister … that is, if Mrs. Dean ever got around to realizing that her younger daughter deserved one.

"Just an idea," Liz had said.

Gritting her teeth, Kate changed the subject and told Holly about Aunt Marion's offer of her cottage for the winter.

"Awesome," Holly said. "That's one problem solved." She gave Kate a high five, then let out an elaborate sigh. "But right now, I've got a bigger one."

"What?"

Holly thrust her algebra homework at Kate. "This."

Figuring out linear equations, Kate decided, was far easier than figuring out her life. She had Holly's problem solved in less than two minutes and was about to dive into her essay on *To Kill a Mockingbird* when her cell phone buzzed with a text from Nathan.

Saw Legend of Sleepy Hollow last night.
xxx Ichabod

Even though Nathan was halfway around the world, he always seemed to sense when Kate needed a boost, like the night he showed up at Mrs. Dean's costume party.

Kate hadn't wanted to go because it was two days before the big Labor Day show, and they should've been cleaning tack and practicing, but Holly talked her into it. Holly had also talked her into a makeover that Kate promptly covered up with her headless horseman outfit. Secretly, she loved her new look but was too embarrassed to share it.

So she hid beneath her voluminous black cloak and wondered how many kids at the party had read the creepy story of Ichabod Crane, while her real-life boyfriend—Nathan Crane—was hiding in the back end of Adam's crazy centaur costume. Kate didn't know he was there till they snagged a picnic table and Nathan had to show himself or risk being sat on by Adam.

It was the best surprise ever.

Two days later, Nathan left for New Zealand to finish filming *Moonlight*—another creepy story—and Kate had no clue when she'd see him again. The other girls envied her for having a movie star boyfriend. To them, it sounded glamorous and exciting, but they had no idea about the frustration and disappointment that went along with it.

Nathan was always thousands of miles away. And even when he was around, they couldn't hang out like other kids because the minute Nathan showed his famous face, he was mobbed by legions of teenage fans.

On top of all that, the gossip mags were forever linking his name with one celebrity after another, especially his blond co-star, Tess O'Donnell.

Kate sighed as she read Nathan's text again. They'd never even been on a real date, and even though Kate really liked him, she was beginning to wonder if she'd be better off with an ordinary guy like Adam Randolph ... or nobody at all.

* * *

On Thursday after school, Kate rode Tapestry over the hunt course until it got too dark to see, then decamped to the indoor arena where they practiced parts of a third-level dressage test Kate had memorized from the USDF's web site.

Tapestry performed brilliantly.

She sailed through a flawless shoulder in and didn't put a foot wrong when Kate asked for a flying change across the diagonal. This was way above Kate's expectations. Leaning forward, she wrapped her arms around Tapestry's sweaty neck and never wanted to let go.

How could she leave this horse behind?

Tapestry's golden ears flicked back and forth as if she understood Kate's turmoil. Tears trickled down Kate's cheeks. She wiped them with her sleeve, but one escaped and landed on Tapestry's silvery mane. It glistened for a moment, then dissolved, just like her life was about to do.

"Drama queen," Kate muttered.

Behaving like a wimp would get her nowhere. She gave herself a shake and thought about Holly who'd spent two years in a wheelchair, unable to walk. She'd never complained about it, either. Right now, Kate's problem was nothing more than a scratch compared to what Holly had endured.

Straightening, Kate gathered up her reins and trotted Tapestry in a small circle, then aimed her at the green-and-white vertical. Tapestry took off, tucked her knees, and soared over the rails as if the fence were no bigger than the toy jumps in Holly's Breyer horse collection. Next came the double oxer, and Tapestry cleared that one as well. She landed gracefully and Kate turned her toward the tricky combination—a triple bar and another vertical with only two strides between them.

A familiar voice trashed her concentration.

"Having a final fling, are you?" came Angela's icy tones.

Kate's joy at riding Tapestry fizzled out. She pulled away from the jumps and wanted to leave but couldn't because Angela and Skywalker stood in the arena's doorway, blocking access to the barn.

"My mother's going to make your father an offer he can't refuse," Angela said, as Kate did her best to squeeze past. "For some reason my stupid little sister wants your horrible horse."

Was this Angela's revenge?

Had she conned her mother into buying Tapestry for Marcia to punish Kate for what happened at the hunter pace? Holly had warned her that Angela was on the warpath, but Kate never expected something like this. Swallowing hard, she shoved her way into the barn and rode Tapestry down the aisle much faster than she usually did.

Angela's scornful laughter followed her.

"Just you wait, Kate McGregor," she said. "I haven't begun to get even yet."

* * *

Kate sobbed out the details to Holly while packing her duffel bag. Blinded by angry tears, she tossed in any old stuff—shorts, t-shirts, and flip-flops—even though Wyoming's fall weather demanded boots, jeans, and a down parka.

"Let me do that," Holly said.

"My father can't sell Tapestry," Kate said between sniffs. "She belongs to me. I'm the registered owner."

Richard North, the Morgan trainer who once owned

Tapestry, had made sure of that. After tracking Kate down, he'd transferred ownership papers to her at the Labor Day show. He was so grateful that Kate had rescued his stolen mare from the slaughterhouse, he'd made a gift of her, with the understanding that Kate allow Tapestry to be bred to his best stallion at some point in the future—like when Kate went off to college—and Richard North would keep the foal.

"Angela's jerking your chain," Holly said. "She's making it all up. Her mother would never buy a horse that belongs to you, so quit freaking out." She folded Kate's green hoodie and laid it on top of her tan corduroys. "How much underwear do you want?"

Kate shrugged. "Who cares?"

"Three sets will do it," Holly said. "You'll be home on Monday. What about socks?" Without waiting for an answer, she scooped up four pairs—gray, two blacks, and a dark blue—from Kate's drawer and stuffed them into her bag. They matched the tops and turtlenecks she'd already chosen for Kate—way more than she needed, of course, and in colors that Holly wouldn't be caught dead in.

Kate's cell phone chirped. She glanced at the screen. *Holly's b'day party. Nov 15?* Adam had texted.

Sure, Kate texted back. It was just over two weeks away. Would she still be around or would she be trying to make a new life without her horse in a place she didn't want to be?

Cool, Adam wrote. *Check w/Liz.*

Kate dropped her phone on the bed. It landed face up amid a pile of textbooks and her discarded summer clothes.

Holly emerged from the bathroom with Kate's cosmetic bag. "Toothbrush, toothpaste, hairbrush, lip gloss—but no makeup," she said. "I didn't think you'd want it."

"Thanks," Kate said.

She stuffed the bag into her duffel's side pocket, then added the latest issue of *Dressage Today*. It would help distract her on the plane. But maybe she'd be better off with something that had nothing to do with horses. She grabbed one of Holly's *Teen Gossip* magazines and stuffed that in as well. A photo of Nathan and Tess O'Donnell was plastered on the front. They were looking at each other across a small table with a candle in the middle.

Holly had told her to ignore it.

So had Nathan. He'd already warned Kate that this picture had been Photoshopped to make it look as if he and Tess were on a romantic date, when in reality, the photos had been taken in two different places, many miles apart.

"Who were you texting with?" Holly said, glancing at Kate's cell phone.

Kate snatched it off the bed. Her messages with Adam were still on full view because she'd forgotten to close the screen. "My, um ... my dad," she said, hoping her blush wouldn't tip Holly off.

Holly gave her an odd look. "He's learned to text?"

Just then, Kate's cell phone sprang into life again, and she almost dropped it. This time it really was her father. Kate shot into the bathroom and closed the door. With luck, Holly would assume she was talking to Nathan.

"Hi," she whispered.

"Can't year you," her father bellowed.

Kate spoke as loud as she dared. "Is everything okay?"

"Change of plans," he said, and Kate listened in stunned silence as her father told her that the Wyoming job had fallen through and he'd be flying to New York in the morning to see a colleague at Columbia University. There was a position in its entomology department that would be perfect for him.

"New York?" Kate said. "As in the *city*?"

"Yes," her father replied. "We'll get an apartment in Manhattan, close to the college and museums. It's going to be a wonderful experience for you, Kate, I promise.

And don't forget to call Aunt Marion and tell her you won't need a ride to the airport."

After he rang off, Kate sat down hard on the edge of Holly's bathtub. If anything, this was worse than Wyoming. At least there were horses out West. The only ones in New York City were police horses and the pitiful nags that pulled carriages around Central Park. They didn't even hold the National Horse Show there any more.

8

To Kate's relief, Holly didn't ask why she'd pretended to be texting with her dad only to have him call her a few seconds later. For now, Adam's birthday surprise for Holly was safe.

"Well, there is *one* good thing about all this," Holly said, after Kate got through explaining her father's change of plans. "Two good things, actually."

"Like what?"

"First, you get to come to Sue's party," Holly said. "And second, New York's a whole lot closer than Wyoming. I bet Mom would let you keep Tapestry here, and you could take the train up on weekends to ride her."

Kate brightened. She hadn't thought of that. If she couldn't talk her father into buying the butterfly museum, living in New York would be a whole lot better than living out West. Not that she had anything against Wyoming. It was just so far away from everything she knew and loved.

"You'll need a Halloween costume," Holly went on.

"And a broom?"

"No," Holly said. "We've given up on that." She rummaged in her messy closet and pulled out the cloak Kate had worn for her headless horseman outfit. "This'll do," she said, giving it a vigorous shake. "Just wear something black underneath it, and you're all set. I think Sue has a spare witch's hat."

"Will I have to put on makeup?" Kate said.

"Duh-uh," Holly said, rolling her eyes. "Even you're not ugly enough to pass for a witch."

Kate laughed and threw a pillow at her.

Holly threw it back. It landed on Kate's bedside lamp and sent it flying. Her water glass tipped over and suddenly they were having a pillow fight and Kate was loving it. Clowning around with Holly took her mind off everything else, like Dad's unsettled plans and Mrs. Dean's threat to make an offer on Tapestry. Saturday was Halloween and they'd go trick-or-treating on horseback. Instead of candy, they would be collecting money for a local horse rescue center.

Liz had already cleared it with the owners.

They'd provided donation boxes along with brochures full of articles and photos for people who wanted to learn more about saving horses. One of the articles featured a ten-year-old boy named Declan who'd won an ASPCA award for helping raise awareness of horse slaughter. Kate shuddered. It wasn't just about dog food any more. People in Europe and Japan were actually eating horse meat.

When feathers began to escape from pillows, Holly called for a truce so they could talk about Sue's party. "Fran's doing our makeup."

"Fran?" Kate said.

"Sue's older sister," Holly explained. "She was a theater major in college, and she's got all the right stuff, like fake warts and false noses and everything."

"Cool," Kate said, rubbing the zit that had appeared on her chin that morning. "If Fran can cover this up, then I'm all over it."

"Leave it alone," Holly said. "Let it ooze."

"Yeah, right," Kate said. "It'll gross everyone out."

"Perfect," Holly said, grinning.

Kate's cell phone buzzed again—another message from Holly's boyfriend. Kate ignored it because if she answered it, Holly would get even more suspicious and wonder why Kate was texting with Adam.

* * *

On Friday afternoon Kate was in the computer lab finalizing her English essay when Angela showed up. She stood beside Kate's cubicle swinging a flash drive from a neon pink ribbon that matched her pink hoodie and the fur trim on her black suede boots.

"Hurry up," she said. "It's my turn."

Kate glanced around the lab. It had ten computers and three were sitting idle. Most kids had their own laptops, but Kate didn't. She always used Holly's, except right now Holly had it with her in class and Kate's homework was due in ten minutes. Ms. Tucker, the English teacher, gave an automatic *F* when assignments were late.

"Go find another computer," Kate said. She saved her document and hit the *print* button.

"I want this one."

"Why?"

"None of your business," Angela snapped.

She elbowed Kate out of the way and plugged in her flash drive. Up came Angela's essay on *To Kill a Mockingbird*. Her English class was an hour later than Kate's, so she still had time to work on it. Kate grabbed her books and glanced at the screen.

Angela covered it with her arms. "Go away."

Kate bit her lip. She had two choices—trade insults with Angela or deliver her essay on time. A no-brainer.

Good grades were way more important than telling Angela to get lost. She snatched her pages from the printer and made it to class with three minutes to spare.

Ms. Tucker smiled as she took Kate's essay. "I look forward to reading this, and I'll need your file as well. It's a new rule," the teacher explained. "So we can check that stuff is original."

"Sure," Kate said. "I'll e-mail it to you after class."

* * *

Adam and Domino were already at the barn when Kate and Holly got home from school. So was Kristina James.

"What's *she* doing here?" Holly muttered.

Adam shrugged. "Angela invited her."

"What for?"

"Halloween, I guess," Adam said. "She said there's a big party at the club or something. She's going with Angela and Courtney."

"They'd better not crash ours," Holly said.

"No worries," Adam said. "Brad and I won't let them." He pulled a goofy face. "We'll be the zombie bouncers."

"Good," Holly said, turning her back on Kristina.

The barn door slid open. Angela and Courtney sauntered toward them pretending to be cool, but when Angela saw Kristina, she squealed like a game show winner. They gave each other air kisses and linked arms. Courtney exclaimed over Kristina's nail polish; Angela admired her lip gloss.

"Is that Strawberry Passion?" she said. "It looks divine."

Adam made a gagging noise.

Kate grinned at him. He was staying at the Pirettis' house for the weekend. He'd promised to help Brad and his father build a haunted house in the ski lodge. Holly said this was a Piretti tradition, and it usually scared everyone to death. On Sunday, Brad and Adam were going snowboarding because the upper slopes had plenty of cover. Somehow, in between all this, Kate had to get him on his own so they could talk about Holly's birthday surprise. So far, all they'd nailed down was the date.

Liz emerged from Skywalker's stall. To Angela, she said, "Your horse has thrown a shoe."

"Then call the farrier," Angela said.

Holly said, "You can't tell my mother what to do."

"Why not?" Angela snapped. "She works here, re-member? It's her job."

For a moment, nobody spoke and Kate wondered if Liz would blast Angela for being rude. But she held on to her temper. She told Angela to leave the barn or pitch in and help with chores. A joke, of course. Angela never did any work, and she certainly wasn't dressed for it. Her silky blue blouse looked like something Kate would wear on a date; that is, if she ever went on one.

Angela gave an indignant snort and strode off, followed by her entourage. They were all giggling.

"Bratface," Holly said, making a fist. "I hate her."

"That's enough," Liz said. "Now, does anyone else need the farrier? He's coming on Monday."

Kate shook her head. Tapestry's hooves were improving, despite having been dry and cracked when she first got her. Careful trimming and good food had helped her heal fast. She looked nothing like the neglected horse Kate had rescued from the auction.

Holly said, "Magician's cool, and I'm going riding. Who's coming?"

"Me," Adam said, hefting his saddle from one arm to the other. "Let's do the hunt course. Domino's in the mood to jump."

"So am I," Kate said. She grabbed a halter and ran outside. Tapestry was in the back paddock with the ponies, sharing a pile of hay. Kate whistled and her mare trotted over.

"Make her lie down," said a small voice behind her.

Startled, Kate turned around. Angela's little sister always managed to surprise her by appearing without warning. Another voice chimed in as Marcia's best friend, Laura Gardner, skipped out of the barn. Her light brown pigtails bounced up and down behind her.

"Please, Kate," she said, eyes shining with excitement.

There really wasn't time, but Kate hated to disappoint the kids. She touched Tapestry's shoulder and pointed at the ground. "Down," she said.

With a soft grunt, Tapestry obeyed. Her forelegs buckled, followed by her hindquarters, and she settled herself into a comfortable heap on the grass. Her brown eyes were full of trust, as if she knew that no harm would come to her as long as Kate was around.

"Can we cuddle her?" Marcia said.

"Sure," Kate said. "But get on your knees first and crawl over. When you're standing up, you look big and frightening to a horse that's lying down."

She squatted by Tapestry's head as the girls followed her instructions. Carefully, they leaned against Tapestry's warm belly. The mare turned her head and whickered at them.

"She wants a treat," Laura said.

Marcia rummaged in her pockets, but came up empty. "I don't have one," she wailed.

"Give her a little hug instead," Kate said. "But be gentle, okay?"

Nodding gravely, Marcia wrapped her skinny arms around Tapestry's neck. Laura snuggled up next to her, and they looked so cute, Kate pulled out her cell phone and took a picture.

Another classic for the barn's Facebook page.

* * *

It wasn't until Holly rode the hunt course that Kate had a chance to get Adam by himself. They jogged side by side along the edge of the field, waiting their turn to jump. Holly had asked them for a critique, but Kate found it hard to concentrate on her and Adam at the same time.

"Okay, so what's the plan?" Kate said, hoping Holly wouldn't demand a detailed analysis of her jumping skills. Not that she needed one. Magician knew this course better than he knew his own stall, and he never put a foot wrong.

Adam shot her a helpless look. "Nothing yet," he said. "But I want to surprise her."

"How?"

He shrugged. "I dunno."

Kate sighed. Typical boy. He had no clue about parties and preparing food and fussing with balloons and table decorations. It was always the girls who handled this sort of stuff. The trouble was, Kate wasn't much good at it herself. She'd never had any practice. That was Holly's talent. She'd be fabulous at organizing her own birthday. Maybe they ought to let her do it.

"Okay," Kate said. "Let's think about what Holly likes."

"That's easy," Adam said, patting Domino's neck. "She likes horses, sparkly stuff, and—"

"—old movies," Kate finished.

He looked thoughtful for a minute. "That's it," he said, slowly. "We'll throw Holly a *Holly*wood party."

"Brilliant," Kate said. "Totally brilliant. She'll love it."

Adam punched the air with his fist so hard that Domino skittered sideways. Then he edged closer to Tapestry and slapped Kate a high five. They were still laughing and congratulating one another when Holly trotted up.

"What are you guys talking about?" she said.

"Nothing," Kate said, shrugging. "Just some stuff about school." Boy, that was *so* lame. Adam didn't even go to their school, plus he was two grades ahead of them.

There was a pause, then Holly said, "So, how did I do?"

"Fabulous," Kate said. "Close to epic."

"Liar," Holly retorted. "You weren't even watching." She rounded on Adam. "Did you see me?"

"Yes," he said. "You were awesome."

Holly held up her hand, fingers splayed. "I made five stupid mistakes, and you idiots missed them all."

"Only five?" Adam said. "I counted six."

"Name it," Holly challenged.

He grinned. "You forgot to smile when you went over the logs."

"My turn," Kate said, hoping to deflect Holly's attention. Any minute now, she'd accuse them of conspiring, which they were. Or worse, she'd be even more suspicious than she already was.

"No, it's mine," Adam said.

Before Kate had a chance to argue, Adam and his paint gelding took off. Kate held her impatient mare in check and watched Holly's boyfriend cruise over the hunt course like it wasn't even there. He flashed a triumphant smile as he jumped the last fence.

"Not bad, huh?" Holly said, sounding proud. She looked at Kate. "Now go out there and do even better, okay?"

Kate relaxed. It seemed as if Holly was back to normal again.

A STORM WOKE THEM AT DAWN the next morning. Rain pounded the roof and a heavy wind rattled the shutters as if it were trying to rip them off.

Holly groaned. "Can witches carry umbrellas?"

"Of course," Kate said. "But in this wind, they'd turn into parachutes." She grabbed her cell phone and punched in the weather app. "They say it's gonna clear up later on, like around three o'clock."

"Good," Holly said, sliding out of bed. "I didn't want to be the Wicked Witch of the Wet." She stuffed her feet into bunny slippers and shuffled off to the bathroom, claiming it was her turn to shower first.

Kate shivered and wrapped herself in Holly's pony print comforter. They'd have to forget about trail riding, and they couldn't ride indoors because Liz would have the arena tied up with lessons till late afternoon. By then, Sue's sister would be transforming them into witches. Kate rubbed her chin. The zit was bigger than ever. It felt like a volcano about to erupt.

Holly had already dubbed it Mount Vesuvius.

* * *

With Robin's help, Kate and Holly stripped stalls, laid down fresh bedding, and swept out the tack room. At noon, Jennifer showed up and got busy decorating everyone's bridles with orange and black ribbons. Sue was at home preparing for the party and trying to keep her brother and Adam from making their haunted house too creepy. She'd forbidden them to use spiders.

"They always do," Holly told Kate. "So be warned."

By three o'clock, Kate was ready to tackle her horse. Tapestry was a mud ball, having been outside all night with the ponies. Her coat was thickening up for the winter, which made it even harder to get the dirt out. In the adjacent stall, Holly curried and brushed Magician, who was marginally less grubby.

"No sense in getting them too clean," Holly said, untangling the knots in Magician's mane. "They're supposed to be faux broomsticks, remember?"

Kate had just finished picking out Tapestry's feet when Adam and Sue arrived with Fran. She set up a table and spread out her makeup. One by one, the kids sat on a metal chair while Sue's talented sister applied grease-paint, warts, and fake noses. She chortled over Kate's zit.

"Awesome," she said, making it look even worse.

Kate stared at herself in the mirror.

A wizened crone with hollow eyes and a hooked nose stared back. Mount Vesuvius had taken over her chin.

Holly said, "Your horse is gonna freak out over this."

"Thanks a bunch," Kate muttered.

But Holly wasn't kidding. It took Kate five minutes and a bag of carrots to convince Tapestry that it really was her beneath the ugly disguise. Domino was even more spooked by Adam's gruesome appearance. He had stitches crawling up his nose, bulging eyeballs, and blood gushing from a mouth full of broken teeth. He could barely talk.

Holly said this was a good thing.

* * *

It had stopped raining by the time Liz handed out donation boxes and flyers. She checked to make sure her team had flashlights and cell phones, and that they were all wearing helmets beneath their pointed hats.

Getting them to stay on was a problem, but Robin had solved it with black duct tape. She'd also stuck yellow reflective tape onto each horse's forelock and tail so they could be seen in the dark from both directions.

"Don't go on anyone's lawn," Liz warned, as riders in long, flowing robes clambered onto their fretful horses. "I don't want angry phone calls tomorrow morning that you've ruined someone's garden."

"We'll be careful, Mom," Holly promised.

A few minutes later, five witches and one zombie rode into Timber Ridge Manor. Tapestry shied at a ghost and almost turned herself inside out when two vampires ran past, cloaks flapping like bat wings. The roads were slick with wet leaves, so nobody dared go faster than a walk.

"We'd better split up," Kate said, patting her nervous horse. "Or we'll be here all night." She was determined to cover as much ground as possible so they'd get lots of money for the rescue center.

Holly and Adam paired off, then Sue and Robin, so Kate teamed up with Jennifer. Beneath her cloak, Jennifer wore green-and-black-striped leggings and ruby slippers she found at the thrift shop.

"Dorothy didn't want them," she told Kate.

Keeping a safe distance, they followed ballerinas, ghouls, and superheroes along sidewalks and up driveways. Excited voices rang out whenever kids spotted the horses. A little girl wearing bunny ears offered Tapestry a plastic carrot. Her elder sister, dressed as a cowgirl, begged Jennifer for a pony ride but backed off when Rebel tried to frisk her for treats.

After crisscrossing the neighborhood, Kate's donation box was stuffed with cash and Jennifer had mysteriously acquired a stash of candy that she promised to share at Sue's party. It was almost time to meet up with the others. But first, they would stop at Jennifer's house.

"Mum's got some yummy treats from England," Jennifer said. "Smarties and Cadbury Flake."

Kate loved them both. "What about pudding?"

"Not this time," Jennifer said, laughing.

Her mother was famous for once inviting Rebel into her kitchen and feeding him vanilla pudding from a bowl. The little kids at the barn loved this. They spoiled the chestnut gelding with tubs of Jell-O pudding until Jen put her foot down and told them her horse would get cavities if they didn't quit.

The Wests' front porch was festooned with fairy lights, carved pumpkins, and pots of cheerful yellow chrysanthemums. Jennifer's mother gave them each a tube of Smarties—England's version of M&Ms—and tucked ten dollars into Kate's donation box. Mr. West added ten dollars more.

"Wow, thanks," Kate said.

The Deans lived next door in a three-story mansion

surrounded by five acres of elaborate landscaping. Jennifer said it wasn't worth going, but Kate was determined. Everyone else had been super generous, so why should Angela's mother get away without donating? She had more money than Donald Trump.

"I'll go," Kate said. "You stay here and wait for the others."

She rode up Angela's long driveway, past an ornamental pond and a formal rose garden. No pumpkins, no lights, and no kids clutching bags of candy. Two stone lions flanked the Dean's portico. A designer wreath bristling with nuts and pine cones adorned the front door, but there was no sign of life behind it. Kate dismounted and knocked. Minutes passed, and she was about to leave when the door cracked open.

"What do you want?" said Mrs. Dean.

Didn't she know it was Halloween?

"Trick or treat?" Kate said. Her hand wobbled as she held out the donation box. "I'm collecting for the horse rescue center."

Mrs. Dean pursed her lips, then disappeared inside. Moments later, she came back and dropped a few coins into Kate's box.

"Keep off my lawn," she said and closed the door.

Riding back down the driveway, Kate made sure she stayed in the middle. No way would she leave one single hoofprint on Mrs. Dean's flowerbeds or her precious grass.

"Told you," Jennifer said, when Kate checked her box.

Angela's mother had donated sixty-two cents.

* * *

Vampire bats and ferocious spiders guarded the Pirettis' front door. Kate stumbled through it and crashed into a skeleton dangling from a rope. She let out a bloodcurdling yell and whipped around, but the others blocked her escape.

"Keep going," Holly said firmly. "It gets worse."

"*Much* worse," Sue warned.

Taking a deep breath, Kate plunged into a maze of tunnels and dead ends. Chains rattled, werewolves howled, and bony fingers plucked at the unwary. A zombie rose from its coffin, and Kate screamed again. She knew it was only Adam, but still—

"Don't stop," Robin whispered.

Fog drifted toward them, swirling around their feet like pond scum. Holding hands, the riding team scurried past the Grim Reaper, narrowly avoided a shark with teeth the size of tombstones, and got totally freaked out by Frankenstein's monster wielding a chainsaw.

"Dude," Jennifer said, slapping him a high five.

Brad groaned. "You recognized me?"

Ramping up their screams, Kate and her friends ran through a curtain of cobwebs and spilled into the Pirettis' rec room. A disco ball spun overhead, music blared from a dozen speakers, and tables overflowed with funky Halloween food—mummified hot dogs, chocolate-dipped owls, and gingerbread skeletons.

Kate took a long drink of glow-in-the-dark apple cider. Being scared to death was thirsty work. Brad the monster lumbered up and dropped a plastic spider in her glass.

"You beast," Kate said, fishing it out.

He grinned. "So, you wanna dance or something?"

With a bolt through his neck and stitches across his massive green forehead, Brad Piretti looked even creepier than she did. Two sets of football pads pumped up his shoulders; his lanky arms protruded from a jacket that was three sizes too small. Awkwardly, they danced to a couple of songs. Brad had a hard time keeping his enormous feet under control. He kept treading on hers. Good thing she still had her riding boots on.

Kate's cell phone chirped.

Boo, said a text from Nathan. *Happy Halloween*.

Kate blushed beneath her makeup. All of a sudden, she felt guilty for dancing with Brad and enjoying it, but it wasn't like she was going to kiss him or anything. She glanced at his mouth—outlined in black—and shuddered. He probably felt the same way about her. Ten minutes later, they won the ugliest couple award—a large can of Silly String.

"This means we're going steady," Brad said.

He pressed the nozzle and sprayed wildly, wrapping them both in a neon green web that he garnished with spiders. Kate tried not to flinch.

"Okay," she said. "Just for tonight."

It was easy to pretend she was someone else when hiding beneath greasepaint, fake warts, and a suffocatingly hot costume. Sweat trickled down her neck. Kate wanted to rip off her scratchy cloak and bulldoze her makeup, but if she did, she'd lose her brave new identity. She'd morph back into being plain old Kate McGregor who was a whole lot more comfortable around horses than she was around boys.

"Let's play kiss-a-witch," Adam said.

"Ugh," said Sue. "Who'd want to kiss *you*?"

"Me," Holly said and brushed her lips against his blood-stained cheek. With a dramatic groan, Adam collapsed on the floor at her feet.

Brad raised his massive brow and looked down at Kate. She'd almost forgotten how cute he was underneath all the goop. His infectious smile, unruly brown curls, and snowboarding skills had turned him into a rock star at school. Maybe one little kiss wouldn't hurt. It wouldn't mean anything because she wasn't Kate, she was—

"The Bride of Frankenstein," Jennifer said.

"Close enough," Holly said, giving Kate a shove.

With a gulp, Kate gathered up her cloak. Brad's platform shoes put him at well over six feet, so she climbed on a chair and planted a kiss on his enormous green forehead. Everyone cheered.

"Way to go," Adam yelled.

Frankenstein gave a lopsided grin and swung Kate to the ground as if she were no heavier than a box of popcorn. Sue cranked up the music and they danced for another hour before racing around the ski lodge on a scavenger hunt, searching for gummy worms, garlic, and fake spiders. Thanks to Brad, there were plenty of those.

"Do you like him?" Holly said.

"Who?"

"Brad, you idiot," Holly said. "Who did you think?"

"He's okay, I guess," Kate said.

Actually, he was better than okay, but she wasn't ready to admit it. She dumped her cloak on a chair. Wisps of hay still clung to her jeans and gray hoodie. There was mud on her boots. The others had brought a change of clothes, but Kate hadn't thought that far ahead.

Holly rolled her eyes. "Fashion plate you are *not*."

Kate yanked off her fake nose and spent the rest of the evening dancing with Brad. He didn't seem to care about her disheveled appearance—or her stupid zit.

* * *

As they were leaving, Adam pulled Kate aside. "I've been thinking," he whispered.

"About Holly's party?" Kate said.

He nodded. "I've got some great ideas."

Kate looked around to make sure Holly wasn't within earshot. "Okay, tell me."

"Movie posters," Adam said. "I bet our local theater has a ton they don't want. We'll hang them on the walls. We can make popcorn, and people could dress up as their favorite stars. We'll put down a red carpet, just like at the Oscars, and—"

"Sshh," Kate warned as Holly ran up. Adam was really on a roll. Kate turned away to hide her grin. She hadn't expected him to be this inventive.

"What are you guys whispering about?" Holly said, shoving Kate's cloak into her arms.

Adam shrugged. "Nothing, just—"

"School?" Holly snapped. "Like last time?"

10

To Kate's relief, Holly didn't quiz her on the ride home. She cracked jokes and teased Kate about Brad as they got ready for bed, but her smile had shifted. It didn't quite reach her eyes. Kate switched off the light. It was easier to hide the truth from Holly in the dark.

They were quiet for a moment, then Holly said, "Are you crushing on my boyfriend?"

"You idiot," Kate said. "Adam's a buddy. He's like a brother."

"So why are you guys always whispering?"

"We're not," Kate said, hoping Holly would back off. "And I've already got a boyfriend, in case you hadn't noticed."

"Then you'd better tell Brad about him."

"I did," Kate said. "At the party."

A sigh wafted over from Holly's bed. "Just promise you don't have a thing for Adam, okay?"

"Cross my heart and hope to die," Kate said.

Tomorrow, she'd text Adam and warn him about Holly's suspicions. From now on, they'd have to be super careful when getting in touch.

"Hmmphh," Holly muttered. "G'night."

Kate fluffed up her pillow and tried to sleep, but her mind was in a muddle over Nathan and she couldn't stop thinking about Brad. He'd asked if she was seeing anyone.

"Kind of," she'd said. "But—"

"That movie guy, huh?"

"Yeah."

Brad gave a shrug and his shoulder pads wobbled. "I thought it was just a dumb rumor."

* * *

A different sort of storm woke Kate and Holly on Sunday morning. Liz thundered into their room and yanked the covers off both beds. Startled, Kate sat bolt upright.

"Mom!" Holly shrieked. "What—?"

"I can't believe you were *so* stupid," Liz fumed.

What had they done now?

Still half asleep, Kate wracked her brain trying to

pinpoint a sin, but nothing came up. She'd half expected Holly to be a little miffed at her, but not Liz as well.

"What did we do?" Holly said, rubbing her eyes. "Scare someone to death?" She lunged for her comforter, but Liz whipped it away. She looked so angry, Kate could almost see steam coming out of her ears.

"No," Liz said. "You ruined Mrs. Dean's lawn." All the breath seemed to leave her body as she slumped onto Holly's bed. "I *told* you to be careful, remember? Not to trample anyone's garden."

"It wasn't me," Holly said. "I didn't go anywhere near Mrs. Dean's house."

Liz rounded on Kate. "Did you?"

"Yes," Kate said. Slowly, she upended her donation box and Mrs. Dean's loose change fell out. "Here's what she gave me."

"That's all?" Holly cried. "The mean old witch."

For a moment or two, Liz stared at the coins on Kate's bed. Finally, she transferred her steely gaze to Kate. "You'd better explain, and it had better be good."

"We all paired up. Jennifer and I trick-or-treated at her house, then I went next door," Kate said, going over each scene in her head to make sure she left nothing out. "But I didn't ride on Mrs. Dean's lawn."

"She says you did," Liz said. "There are hoofprints all over it, and you destroyed her favorite rose bushes as well." She groaned. "I'm afraid it's your word against hers."

Kate's heart got stuck in her throat. Challenging Mrs. Dean was like fighting a brush fire with squirt guns—nobody won and everyone got burned.

"Ask Jennifer," Holly said. "She rode with Kate."

"Not to the Deans'," Kate said. "She told me it was a waste of time so I went by myself. Jennifer waited in the road."

This was turning into a nightmare. First, Holly was suspicious of her and Adam; now Liz was accusing her of something she didn't do. What came next? The plague? Rats? An algebra test she'd forgotten to study for?

"Call her anyway," Holly said.

Kate punched in Jennifer's number. Mrs. West answered and said that Jennifer had gone out with her dad. She'd be back later that night. "Can I help you with anything?" she added.

"Thanks, but no," Kate said, and hung up.

"Now what?" Holly said.

She looked at Kate, question marks written all over her face.

* * *

Feeling like an outcast, Kate trudged to the barn. She'd given up trying to convince Liz she was innocent.

Nobody else besides the Timber Ridge team had gone trick-or-treating on horseback, and Kate was the only one who'd actually ridden up the Deans' driveway. The evidence against her was overwhelming.

Liz had insisted she apologize to Mrs. Dean and offer to pay for damages; then she'd left for a dressage clinic and dropped Holly at Sue's house on the way. Mr. Piretti had promised her a ride in the gondola and Holly was super excited. She'd get to see Adam and Brad snowboarding on the mountain's upper slopes. She invited Kate to tag along, but Kate had the uneasy feeling Holly didn't want her, so she begged off.

The barn echoed with emptiness.

Except for Skywalker, the horses were all outside. Angela's bay gelding stood in the cross ties while Marcia brushed dried mud off his legs. He gave Kate a baleful look, as if bored by the attention.

"Are you gonna ride Tapestry?" Marcia said.

Her voice was so quiet that Kate had to lean closer. Marcia's face reddened, and she looked away like she was embarrassed or hiding something.

"What's wrong?" Kate said.

Marcia shrugged. "Nothing." There was a pause. "You were really scary last night."

"You saw me?" Kate said, surprised.

The Deans' house had looked half deserted. There

was no sign of Angela and Courtney, who were probably at the Timber Ridge club house with Kristina James.

"Yes," Marcia said. "I was upstairs, and—"

"You weren't out trick-or-treating?"

Marcia gave another shrug. "Mom says it's stupid."

Kate clenched her fists. She wanted to punch Mrs. Dean on the nose. Angela went to a fancy Halloween party, but her younger sister had to stay home, locked away like Cinderella.

A tear rolled down Marcia's cheek. Then another. She dropped her brush and slumped onto a tack trunk. "I want my real mom," she wailed and buried her face in her hands.

Real mom?

Kate sat beside her. She wasn't much good at comforting people. Feeling awkward, she took Marcia's hand and squeezed it. Skywalker snorted and stamped his foot. He'd thrown another shoe.

"You have a mother," Kate said, not knowing what else to say. It sounded feeble the moment the words left her mouth.

"She's my stepmother," Marcia sobbed.

Astonished, Kate tore her eyes from Skywalker and looked at Angela's sister. All of a sudden Marcia's frizzy red hair, brown eyes, and freckles made sense. Maybe she looked like her father. Kate had never even met Mr.

Dean. He had a big-wig job in New York and didn't come home very often.

As if reading her mind, Marcia said, "My dad married Angela's mother when I was two." She took a ragged breath. "They told me to keep it a secret. Don't tell anyone, please."

"I promise," Kate said, getting to her feet. She unclipped Skywalker from the cross ties and said, "Would you like to ride Tapestry again?"

* * *

Marcia did so well with Tapestry that Kate let her off the lunge line. After they trotted a few circles, Kate told her to canter. Marcia eased Tapestry back to a walk, then urged her forward. She didn't even bounce in the saddle and had a far better seat than her sister did. Tapestry's ears flicked back and forth—a good sign. It meant she was listening to her rider.

"Nice," Kate called out. "Now lower your hands."

Marcia nodded. She cantered another circle, then transitioned into a working trot and picked up the correct diagonal right away—something that Angela often got wrong.

Watching her ride, Kate thought about Marcia's startling outburst. Was Marcia's mother still alive? Had she died when Marcia was a baby, or had she run off and abandoned her? Kate shivered. She felt a surge of sympathy for the poor little kid.

* * *

Marcia hung around while Kate schooled Tapestry over fences. She darted around the arena, adjusting poles and putting them back up whenever Tapestry knocked them down. Afterward, she helped Kate cool the mare off and groomed her with the same care and devotion she showered on Skywalker.

Kate had two hours until evening feed.

"I'll walk you home," she told Marcia, as they turned Tapestry loose in the back paddock. Maybe she could talk to Mrs. Dean and explain that she wasn't the one who wrecked the front lawn.

Marcia bit her lip. "Okay."

Ten minutes later, Kate gasped when she saw the mess. Mrs. Dean's finely manicured grass looked as if someone had held a horse show on it. Clods of mud stuck up like miniature volcanoes, skid marks ran in all directions, and uprooted rose bushes lay strewn about. There were hoofprints everywhere.

"I gotta go," Marcia said and ran off.

Kate wanted to step on the grass, but she didn't dare. It was still wet and muddy and her boots would leave telltale marks. Planting her feet firmly on the driveway, she knelt down for a closer look at the trampled lawn.

She touched a hoofprint and traced the edge with her finger. It had the distinct outline of a metal shoe, but the one beside it didn't. Its imprint was the entire hoof, including the V-shaped frog. Whatever horse made this print was missing a shoe.

Kate rocked back on her heels.

All the barn's horses had a full set of shoes—except Skywalker. But that was insane. Why would his hoofprints show up on Mrs. Dean's lawn when Angela hadn't even been out trick-or-treating? Kate was about to reach for her phone to take pictures when a silver Mercedes pulled up.

Mrs. Dean rolled down her window. "What are *you* doing here?"

"Revisiting the scene of her crime," said Angela.

Giggles erupted from the back seat. Through the car's tinted glass, Kate could see Courtney and Kristina James. Angela's cousin stuck out her tongue like a bratty toddler. Kristina wrinkled her nose.

"Mrs. Dean," Kate said, trying to keep her voice steady. "I'm sorry about your lawn, but I didn't do it."

"Hah!" Angela said. "So who did? The Four Horsemen of the Apocalypse? My Little Pony?"

More giggles erupted, and Kate wanted to hurl accusations at Angela, but her only evidence was a couple of hoofprints. She really needed to take a photo of them before it got dark.

Mrs. Dean said, "I'll be sending you a bill for the repairs."

"Hope you've got lots of money," Angela said.

The moment Mrs. Dean's garage door closed, Kate fumbled for her cell phone, then realized with horror that she'd left it at the barn. She stared at the hoofprints. If it rained again, they'd be turned to mush.

Could she sneak back to take a photo?

Angela and Courtney would probably stake out the front yard to make sure that she didn't.

11

Horses snorted with impatience as Kate scooped grain into their buckets. She added vitamins, checked salt blocks, and was splitting a bale of hay when Holly raced into the barn, bubbling over about Adam's snowboarding adventures. Breathlessly, she told Kate he'd even tried the half-pipe with Brad, who was seriously good at it.

"It's like they were flying," Holly said, waving her arms in circles. "I got dizzy, just watching them." She scooped up a flake of hay and dumped it into Magician's stall.

Grabbing the hose, Kate began to fill water buckets.

"There'll be tons of new snow this week," Holly went on. "Brad says a big storm is coming. The guys can't wait."

"Snow?" Kate said. "Isn't it kind of early for that?"

"Not in Vermont," Holly said. "We had a blizzard at Halloween last year." She dumped more hay in Skywalker's stall and peered over his door. "Did he lose another shoe?"

"Yes," Kate said. She topped up Tapestry's water, then turned to face Holly. "You're not gonna believe this, but I didn't trash Mrs. Dean's lawn. Angela did."

"Angela?" Holly said. "You've got to be kidding."

"No, I'm dead serious," Kate said.

Holly sat down hard on an upturned muck bucket. "Tell me."

Quickly, Kate ran through her evidence—the bare hoofprints on Mrs. Dean's lawn and Marcia brushing mud off Skywalker's legs. "He was in the barn all week and nobody rode him, so where did the mud come from?"

"Mrs. Dean's garden?" Holly said.

Kate nodded. "Angela must've galloped over it after her parents went to bed. Mrs. Dean probably told her I'd been to their house and Angela saw a chance to get even."

"At midnight," Holly muttered, "with Courtney's help."

"And Kristina's," Kate said.

This was Angela's worst revenge ever. The others had been childish and spiteful, but this one could cost Kate and her dad a lot of money. Even worse, he might lose faith in Kate and really put his foot down about selling Tapestry.

"How can you prove it?" Holly said.

Kate held up her cell phone. "By taking a photo of Skywalker's hoofprint. I didn't have this with me today, so I'm going back tomorrow after school."

"Better yet," Holly said. "Make a plaster cast."

Kate hadn't even thought of that.

"It'd be like those crime scene shows on TV," Holly said. "You could show it to the farrier, and he'd identify Skywalker's foot." She clapped her hands. "Case closed, easy-peasy."

"Yeah, right," Kate said. "I can just see us messing with plaster of Paris on Mrs. Dean's front lawn while Angela and Courtney are watching."

"Then let's find Skywalker's shoe," Holly said. "I bet he threw it while Angela was jerking him around her mother's precious garden."

The barn door slid open, and Liz stepped inside.

"Don't tell your mom about this," Kate whispered, dropping the last flake of hay into Daisy's stall. The pinto mare stuck her nose into it eagerly. "Not till we get some evidence, okay?"

"My lips are zipped," Holly said.

* * *

By lunch time on Monday, the school was buzzing with rumors about the vandalism on Mrs. Dean's lawn. Kate could feel a hundred pairs of eyes watching her as she stood in line at the cafeteria. Holly said she wouldn't be surprised if Kate got hauled into the principal's office again.

"You're a big help," Kate said, reaching for a burger.

Holly nudged her. "Only kidding."

The summons Holly had joked about arrived halfway through Kate's study hall, except it didn't come from Mrs. Gordon.

"Ms. Tucker wants to see you," said a familiar voice.

Taken by surprise, Kate looked up.

Brad Piretti grinned down at her. Even without his football pads, he looked enormous. He also looked devastatingly cute without all that yucky makeup.

"She sent me to find you," he said.

"What for?"

"Dunno." Brad shrugged. "Hey, it was fun the other night."

"Yeah," Kate said, gathering up her books. Ms. Tucker probably didn't get the text file she'd e-mailed on Friday. Good thing she had her essay on *To Kill a Mockingbird* backed up on a thumb drive in her knapsack.

"Her office is on the second floor," Brad said.

"Thanks," Kate said and took the stairs two at a time.

After waving Kate into her cramped office, Ms. Tucker shut the door and cleared space on a chair for Kate to sit down. Notebooks and papers crowded the teacher's desk; a coffee can wrapped in multicolored yarn held a forest of red pencils.

Kate pulled out her thumb drive. "Here's my file."

"I already have it," Ms. Tucker said. She laid a hand on the nearest pile of paper and looked at Kate, eyes narrowed behind her rimless glasses. "Do you know what plagiarism is?"

"I think so," Kate said. "It's when you take someone else's words or ideas and present them as your own."

"Like this?" Ms. Tucker said and held up Kate's essay.

It had a huge red X on the first page.

* * *

In growing disbelief, Kate listened to Ms. Tucker explain how she'd run Kate's file through an online validation system and discovered that a major portion of Kate's essay already existed in its database.

"Which means," Ms. Tucker said, "you copied it from somewhere else."

"I didn't," Kate said, as tears sprang to her eyes.

"That essay is mine, all mine." She'd labored over every word and had driven Holly mad by reading it to her out loud more than once.

There was a pause, then Ms. Tucker said, "I believe you, Kate. I don't think you cheated, but the software does and that's what we have to deal with." She picked up a red pencil and twirled it between her chubby fingers. "Do you have any notes, something to show me how you did your research?"

"I've got tons of notes," Kate said, sniffing.

Ms. Tucker handed her a tissue. "Electronic?"

Kate nodded. They were on Holly's laptop—unless she or Holly had deleted them. Kate couldn't remember. So much had happened since Friday.

"Good," Ms. Tucker said. "They'll help prove your work is original." She opened a drawer and tucked Kate's essay inside. "I'm keeping this quiet for now, but be sure to e-mail me those files by end of school tomorrow. Otherwise, I'll have to tell Mrs. Gordon and I'm afraid it will go on your transcript."

Kate gulped. "Will I be suspended?"

"Let's not go there yet, okay?"

* * *

"It's a computer flub-up," Holly said. "You're the last person in the world who'd cheat." She threw her knapsack onto the bus, climbed in after it, and claimed the front seat.

Kate squeezed in beside her.

"I bet you don't even know *how* to cheat," Holly went on, "unless you've been taking lessons from Angela."

"Every Thursday," Kate deadpanned.

Holly's giggles lifted Kate's spirits. They lifted again five minutes later when her father called to say things hadn't gone the way he hoped in New York and that he'd be coming up next weekend to talk about their options.

"Maybe he'll take another look at the butterfly museum," Holly said, slapping Kate a high five, "*and* my mother."

"Dream on," Kate said, feeling herself blush.

But Holly was right. This would solve all her problems. Well, almost. First, she had to clear herself of plagiarism and lawn destruction.

* * *

The bus let them off at Holly's house. It had gotten a lot colder, so they changed into fleece hoodies, down vests, and their warmest breeches before they headed for the Deans' house. Kate wanted to take photos and find Skywalker's missing shoe before Angela and Courtney got home from cheerleading practice. Mrs. Dean would be at the club playing tennis till five, so the coast was clear.

Except for Marcia.

She zoomed out of the driveway on her bike and missed them by inches. Kate watched her skid around the corner and pedal furiously toward the barn as if she were on some sort of mission. Her red parka made a vivid splash against the bare trees.

"Oh, no," Holly said. She grabbed Kate's arm.

Kate turned around. "What's wrong?"

"That," Holly said, pointing.

Earth moving equipment rumbled over Mrs. Dean's front lawn. Bulldozers pushed, backhoes scooped, and a platoon of landscapers unrolled turf that was greener than fake grass. Two men dug holes for new rose bushes; another raked dirt into neat little furrows.

Appalled, Kate stared at them.

Metal monsters the size of dinosaurs had churned her evidence into oblivion. Gone were the hoofprints, the skid marks, and Skywalker's shoe. They were buried beneath six inches of new top soil and mulch.

"C'mon," Holly said. "Let's go and find Mom. We need her help."

"She's gone to that seminar at Larchwood, remember?"

Holly groaned. "I forgot."

"Now what?" Kate said. Without a photo of Skywalker's hoofprint—or his missing shoe—she was doomed. Nobody, except Holly, would believe that she hadn't trashed Mrs. Dean's lawn.

"We'll think of something," Holly said.

A chill wind whipped Kate's hair into a froth. She zipped up her hoodie and glanced at the mountain. Heavy clouds shrouded its peak. The lower slopes were barely visible. Maybe Brad was right and snow was on the way.

* * *

Skywalker's empty stall didn't register with Kate till she'd finished grooming Tapestry. "Where is he?"

"Outside?" Holly said, brushing Magician's tail.

On their way into the barn, Kate hadn't noticed Angela's horse in the back paddock or the riding ring, but she hadn't been paying much attention. Curious, she pocketed her hoof pick and checked the tack room. All the saddles were lined up neatly on their racks—except for Skywalker's. His bridle was missing, too. Feeling uneasy, she walked back to Holly.

"His tack is gone, so someone's riding him."

"Oh, get real," Holly said, running a body brush

over Magician's shiny rump. "Angela's at school waving pom-poms, and nobody else is allowed to ride Skywalker except Mom and she's not here."

"Then where—?"

"Chill out," Holly said. She rolled her eyes and peered at Kate through the bars of Magician's stall. "He's probably in the top pasture with Daisy, and Angela has taken her saddle home to clean it."

"Angela? Cleaning tack?" Kate said. "You can't be serious."

"Well, Marcia, then," Holly replied. "She always does it, anyway."

A dozen light bulbs went off in Kate's head—Marcia always begging to ride Skywalker, her anger toward Mrs. Dean, and her zooming out of the driveway on her bike and almost knocking them over.

"Marcia," Kate said. "I bet she's got him."

"Before you go ballistic," Holly said, "check her bike."

Kate raced for the wash bay, where all the kids left their bicycles in cold weather. And there was Marcia's— lying on its side like Mrs. Dean's uprooted rose bushes. In a flash, Kate turned and ran toward the indoor arena. Its double doors yawned open, but there were no lights, no hooves pounding the tanbark, and certainly no Skywalker. This meant Marcia was riding him outside.

But where? Had she gone on the trails?

Ducking into the tack room, Kate grabbed her saddle and bridle and Holly's, too. They had an hour to find Marcia before it got dark.

12

KATE HAD JUST FINISHED tightening Tapestry's girth when the mare pricked her ears and neighed.

"What is it, girl?" Kate said.

With an almighty crash, Skywalker exploded into the barn. Nostrils flaring, he thundered down the aisle. Sparks flew from his hooves. His empty saddle hung halfway around his belly, and a stirrup had gone missing.

"Oh, no," Holly cried. "Where's Marcia?"

The frantic horse skidded to a stop, whirled around, and showed the whites of his eyes. Kate shot a worried look toward the arena. Its doors were still open. She had to catch Skywalker before he got loose in there.

"It's okay, boy," she murmured.

He sniffed warily at the carrot she held out, then took a step toward her and lipped it up.

"Good boy," Kate said, taking his reins.

Holly opened the door to Skywalker's stall. He bolted inside, dragging Kate with him. She whipped off his tack. There was no time to cool him down, so Holly thrust a blanket at her. She threw it over Skywalker's sweaty back and fastened the buckles. With luck, it would help prevent him from colicking or tying up.

"Phone your mom," Kate said, "and Mrs. Dean."

While Holly made calls, Kate ransacked Liz's office for a flashlight. After two duds, she found one that worked. Its weak beam fluttered over the barn walls, but it was better than nothing.

What else would they need?

Her eyes landed on a dusty old blanket. Marcia might be hurt or in shock, and she'd certainly be cold. Kate shook out the blanket, then rolled it up and tied it to her saddle with baling twine.

"C'mon, let's go," Holly said.

Kate swung herself into Tapestry's saddle. "Did you reach Liz?"

"Nope," Holly said, as they rode outside. "Didn't get Mrs. Dean, either."

"What about Angela?"

"Voice mail," Holly said. "I left messages."

"Then let's call Mr. Piretti," Kate said.

"Good idea," Holly said. "He'll know what to do."

As she pulled out her phone, a gray pickup trundled into the parking lot. A huge horseshoe was bolted to its front fender. It stopped in front of the barn doors, and out climbed a man wearing a leather apron.

"It's George," Holly said. "I forgot he was coming."

The farrier's friendly smile turned into a frown when Holly explained what was going on. They swapped cell numbers, and George promised to stick around till Liz got back. In the meantime, he'd trim the ponies and keep an eye on Skywalker to make sure he was okay.

"Don't forget his new shoes," Holly said.

George tipped his hat. "Ayuh."

* * *

They rode single file through the woods, scouring the ground for tracks. Now and then, Skywalker's bare hoofprints appeared, but it was hard to isolate them among all the others. The sky darkened, and it began to snow.

"Oh great," Holly said.

Shivering, Kate zipped up her vest. Snowflakes, as pretty as Christmas ornaments, drifted down and frosted Tapestry's mane. For a moment, Kate felt as if they were inside a snow globe. If this kept up, the ground would be covered in less than ten minutes, and whatever tracks Skywalker had left behind would vanish.

"Now what?" Holly said. "Should we split up?"

"No," Kate said. "Call your mom again."

But it was probably useless. Cell coverage on the mountain was notoriously unreliable, especially in bad weather. At least Holly had gotten hold of Mr. Piretti before they left the barn. He and Brad would begin searching right away.

Holly shook her cell phone. "No signal."

"Okay," Kate said. "Let's think about this logically. Skywalker's saddle was missing a stirrup, which means Marcia fell off. She didn't dismount."

"Right," Holly said. "So, something must've spooked him."

"But what?" Kate said. "And where?"

There were dozens of things to spook a horse on the trails—rocks, tree stumps, a twig snapping underfoot. Horses sometimes spooked for no reason at all. In the distance, something rumbled.

"Thunder?" Kate said.

Holly frowned. "It sounds like the gondola."

She urged her horse into a trot, and Kate followed. They couldn't go much faster because the ground was getting slick. Magician's hooves churned up clods of wet leaves. Tapestry side-stepped, and Kate ducked to avoid a low-hanging branch already laden with snow.

Half of it went down her neck.

The trail spilled into a long, sloping meadow. Lift towers marched up the middle. Cables whined and wheels rattled as empty gondola pods rumbled overhead like brightly colored Easter eggs. Whirls of snow blew off their curved roofs. Tapestry snorted and skittered sideways.

"Easy, girl," Kate said, patting her neck.

As they walked their nervous horses beneath the ski lift, Holly pointed to a blue-and-yellow gondola. "I was in one of those yesterday. You can see for miles, and you wouldn't believe how much snow Mr. Piretti's machines have made," she said. "The half-pipe's on the other side of this hill, but I seriously doubt Marcia rode up there."

"How about the hunt course?" Kate said.

Had Marcia gone there to prove she was good enough to ride Skywalker? Her sister was always showing off about how successful she was at jumping the Timber Ridge hunt course. It was around here somewhere, but Kate had lost all sense of direction.

Holly pulled out her crumpled trail map. She studied it for a moment, then said, "The quickest way is straight through those trees over there. I think there's a path."

"What's the alternative?"

"There isn't one," Holly said, checking her map again. "Unless we go halfway back to the barn and start all over from another direction."

"Okay, let's go," Kate said.

"Through the woods?"

Kate nodded. They didn't have time for a detour.

* * *

Fir trees and pines formed a dense canopy over the trail and shielded them from the worst of the storm. Every sound was muffled, even that of the horses' hooves as they crunched on dead leaves and snow. Kate felt as if they were riding through a tunnel, and she was reaching for her flashlight when Holly asked the question that had been on Kate's mind ever since they left the barn.

"Why did Marcia run off with Skywalker?"

"Because—" Kate replied, then caught her breath.

Did she have the right to betray Marcia's confidence? She already felt guilty for encouraging Marcia to ride Tapestry. If she hadn't, Angela's little sister might not have had the guts to ride Skywalker, and they wouldn't be out looking for her right now.

"What aren't you telling me?" Holly said.

Kate rode up beside her. "Marcia's angry and upset. I think she's done this to punish her mother. She's, like, totally mad at her."

"Hah," Holly said. "We're *all* mad at Mrs. Dean. That's nothing new."

"I know," Kate said quietly. "But this is different."

A gust of wind whipped snow off the trees like feathers from a pillow. Tapestry tossed her head. Magician snorted and tried to turn around. Holly pulled him back on track.

"Different?" she said. "How?"

Hating herself for breaking a promise, Kate told Holly what she knew, which wasn't much. Marcia hadn't said another word after blurting out her story. In the middle of a cold, dark forest it sounded more like a Grimm's fairy tale than ever, right down to a wicked stepmother, an absentee father, and an evil sister who put Cinderella's ugly stepsisters to shame.

"Poor kid," Holly said. "I wonder if Mom knows."

"I doubt it," Kate said. "This is the Deans' family secret."

Moments later, the woods opened up and they rode onto the hunt course. Snow drifts had turned the jumps into odd shapes that looked like furniture shrouded with dust sheets. Marcia's red jacket should make her easy to find. Against the snow, it would show up as bright and clear as Little Red Riding Hood's cloak.

Holly suggested they split up.

She took the upper end of the course, while Kate rode toward the bottom. They'd meet in the middle and then circle the perimeter in opposite directions. There were plenty of places for a frightened child to hide among the shrubs and trees that bordered the field.

Head down, Tapestry plowed steadily through the snow. Kate couldn't get over how much had fallen in such a short time. She tightened her grip and whispered to Tapestry who flicked her ears as if to say, *I know what I'm doing.* According to her previous owner, she'd been born in a blizzard. Tapestry was used to this sort of weather.

At the lower part of the course, Kate turned and headed back up the middle. She checked each jump as they trudged past, but there was no sign of a red jacket or anything else that would show Marcia was here. No tracks, either.

Abruptly, Tapestry halted.

Lost in thought, Kate almost fell off. She hauled herself back into the saddle. Tapestry quivered and let out a neigh. Kate tried to urge her forward, but the mare wouldn't move.

"What's wrong?" Kate said, looking around.

Holly rode out of the gloom. "Did you hear it?"

"No," Kate said. "What—?"

"Coyote," Holly said. "Listen."

An eerie howl filled the air, and Kate's blood ran cold. Her irrational fears about fairy tales, wolves, and

Little Red Riding Hood had just turned frighteningly real.

* * *

Holly said coyotes didn't attack people, but Kate wasn't convinced. Marcia was a small kid. If she was injured and the coyote smelled blood, it might turn on her.

Rather than split up again, they rode around the perimeter, checking snow-covered bushes and remnants of stone walls. Every two minutes, Holly tried her cell phone and got nowhere. Kate didn't even bother with hers. Its battery had gone dead.

The horses heard it first—a feeble cry that sounded like an abandoned kitten. Ears on full alert, Magician and Tapestry raised their heads and snorted.

"Marcia?" Kate yelled.

Holly cupped her mouth with both hands. "Where are you?" she bellowed.

Back came another cry, louder this time.

"Over there," Kate said, pointing, "by the brush jump."

Its forest of dead twigs stuck up through the snow like a bad haircut. Holly got there first. She flung herself off Magician and crouched on the ground. Pulling out her flashlight, Kate shone it on Marcia, curled up in her red jacket.

"It hurts," she cried, clutching her shoulder.

With fumbling fingers, Kate untied the blanket and wrapped it carefully around Marcia. Her lips were pinched and bloodless; her face almost blue with cold. She shivered and gave Kate a fearful look. Had she heard the coyote?

Holly said, "Let's get Marcia onto Tapestry."

"No," Kate said. "She's injured, and we could make things worse." This much she remembered from a first aid course she'd taken in fourth grade: *Don't move the victim unless you know what you're doing.*

"Then we'd better get help," Holly said.

"You go," Kate said. "I'll stay with Marcia."

Anxiously, she watched Holly clamber onto Magician and ride off. Maybe her cell phone would pick up a signal before she reached the barn.

"I'm freezing," Marcia whispered.

Kate tore off her gloves and slipped them onto Marcia's cold hands. The little girl couldn't stop shaking. Kate doubled up the blanket, but it wasn't enough. What else could she use? A half-remembered film about survival shot into her mind. Something to do with body heat. Tapestry lowered her velvety nose and nuzzled them. Her breath warmed Kate's face.

That was it! A fuzzy, four-legged blanket.

Kate scrambled to her feet. She pulled off Tapestry's

saddle and pointed at her shoulder. "Down girl," she said. "Down."

Tapestry hesitated, then dropped to her knees. With a grunt, she collapsed. Waves of snow cascaded around her like a fountain. Kate helped Marcia snuggle against the mare's warm belly and covered them both with the blanket. Marcia groaned when Kate accidentally bumped her shoulder. It was probably dislocated, or else she'd broken her collar bone.

"Where did you fall off?" Kate said.

"H-h-here."

"Jumping the brush?"

Marcia nodded, and Kate whistled through her teeth. This kid had more guts than brains, but Kate couldn't help but admire her. She wanted to give Marcia a big hug, but she didn't dare because of the shoulder. Carefully, Kate leaned forward and removed the stirrup from Marcia's boot. It was really jammed on, probably because of the way she landed.

The coyote yowled again, and Marcia whimpered.

"He won't bother us," Kate said, wishing she felt as confident as she sounded. "And if he tries, Tapestry will bite him."

"And kick him?" Marcia said.

"You bet," Kate agreed. "She'll chase him off."

A big lie, of course.

Horses ran away from danger. They didn't face it head on unless they were stallions defending their mares. Kate wracked her brains for ways to distract Marcia and came up with *Moonlight*. All the barn kids loved that book. They especially loved hearing about Kate's adventures on the movie set, and she'd just gotten through describing how she'd ridden bareback in her screen test when Marcia interrupted.

She said, "I saw Angela do it."

"Do what?"

"Trash Mom's lawn," Marcia said. "My stupid sister galloped Skywalker all over it. I found his shoe."

Kate hardly dared to speak. "Have you still got it?"

"Yes," Marcia said, her voice barely above a whisper. "I hid it under my bed."

All of Kate's breath came out in a rush. Her head spun with the implications of this—not the least of which was whether anyone would believe Marcia even if she did produce Skywalker's missing shoe. It could be any one of a dozen he'd thrown in the last year.

13

MINUTES PASSED, or maybe hours. Kate couldn't tell. Her brain had morphed into ice cubes, and all she could think about was hot chocolate, a blazing fire, and down quilts.

She blew on her hands, then shoved them inside her vest and wished she could shove her frozen toes in there as well. Her tall leather boots were designed for riding, not for keeping warm. The coyote howled again, its forlorn cry muffled by falling snow.

"Don't worry," Kate whispered, more for her own sake than Marcia's. "He's far away."

Marcia's head tilted to one side.

Gently, Kate fluffed up the blanket and settled the sleeping girl against her shoulder. Whatever else, she had to keep both of them as warm as possible. Like a mother hen clucking over her chicks, Tapestry whickered and nudged Kate with her whiskery nose as if to make sure they were both okay.

A glow of pride drove the chill from Kate's bones.

Would any other horse do this—lie down in a snowstorm to protect a couple of kids? If someone wrote this scene in a book, readers would scoff and say it couldn't happen. Even Kate had to admit she'd have a hard time believing it if she hadn't seen it for real.

In the distance, lights wavered.

Kate blinked and looked again, but the lights vanished. Clearly, she was hallucinating. A few moments later, they appeared again, darting about like giant fireflies. Then came the roar, and all of a sudden, two snowmobiles blasted through the snow and skidded to a stop. Their headlights almost blinded her.

Shielding her eyes with one arm, Kate held onto Marcia with the other as Tapestry lurched to her feet. The mare shook herself vigorously and showered Kate with snow. Two figures leaped off the snowmobiles.

"Kate, are you all right?" Brad said. His voice rose above the engines, idling now, but still deafening after all the cold silence.

Shivering, Kate said, "Yes, but Marcia's hurt. Be careful with her."

"Dad's an EMT," Brad said, as his father crouched beside Marcia. "He knows what to do."

The rescue sled was piled with blankets, pillows, and flasks of hot chocolate. Kate drank hers thirstily. "Where's Holly?" she said, wiping her mouth.

"In the barn," Brad said, "making phone calls."

"What about Liz?"

"She's on her way home," Brad said, raising his goggles.

The only bits of him Kate could see were his anxious green eyes peering at her between the frosted rim of his ski cap and the scarf that wound over his nose and mouth like a snowman's muffler. His black mittens were the size of boxing gloves. He yanked another pair from his backpack and pulled them over Kate's frozen hands.

She looked at Marcia, still half-conscious, being laid on the sled and wrapped in blankets. Carefully, Mr. Piretti strapped her down.

"Did anyone get hold of Mrs. Dean?"

"Last I heard, Holly was still trying," Brad said.

His father jumped onto the lead snowmobile, revved its engine, and sped back into the night. It swallowed Marcia and the rescue sled like a black hole.

Brad produced a small, powerful flashlight and helped Kate find her saddle, half buried in snow. Wiping it off, she wondered how much saddle soap it would take to reclaim the soggy leather. She was about to place it on

Tapestry's back, but changed her mind. The mare had already done enough. She didn't need to be carrying a heavy wet saddle as well.

Feeling enormously proud of her horse, Kate kissed Tapestry's velvety nose, then shook out the blanket Marcia had been wrapped in and draped it over the mare's back. It wasn't nearly big enough to cover her, but it was better than nothing and would help keep her from getting chilled on the long walk home.

"I'll come with you," Brad said, hefting Kate's saddle onto one arm as if it weighed no more than a hand towel.

Kate pointed at his snowmobile. "What about that?"

"It can stay here. I'll come and get it later." He pulled off his scarf and wrapped it around Kate's neck. "That is, if I can find it."

Already, his machine was half covered with snow.

* * *

To steady herself, Kate held onto Tapestry's mane and stumbled beside her, trying to keep her frozen feet clear of the mare's hooves. Not that it would matter if Tapestry stepped on them ... Kate's toes were beyond numb.

When they reached the end of the hunt course, Kate scrunched up her eyes. Stiffly, she turned around and looked at the snow-covered jumps, barely visible in the gloom. It was hard to believe she'd ridden over them just three days before.

It seemed like a lifetime ago.

Her foot struck something hard and she tumbled forward. The snowy ground rushed up and she felt herself being yanked upright again.

"You okay?" Brad said.

"Yeah," Kate muttered. "But I can't feel my feet." She limped a couple of steps. "I'll be okay, long as I keep moving."

"No," Brad said. "You need to ride." He cupped a massive hand around Kate's left knee and lifted her onto Tapestry's back before she had a chance to argue. "You probably don't have frostbite, at least not yet. But if you do, walking will make it worse."

Balancing Tapestry's saddle on one knee, Brad pulled more stuff from his knapsack—a pair of huge fuzzy socks covered with some sort of silvery foil. Slowly, he eased off Kate's boots and slipped the socks over her frozen feet.

"These'll help," he said. "And soak your feet in warm water when you get home. Not hot, okay? That would really hurt."

How did he know about all this?

Then Kate remembered that Brad was part of the Timber Ridge ski patrol team. He was also a champion snowboarder and his father was a volunteer firefighter. Awkwardly, she grasped Tapestry's reins. Her fingers were beginning to thaw, thanks to Brad's mittens.

"You going to Holly's party?" he said.

She'd forgotten all about it. Two weeks from now, she could be living miles away or back home in Connecticut helping her dad pack up the condo. "I don't know," she said. "Maybe."

"What about your boyfriend?" Brad said. "Is he coming?"

"He's in New Zealand," Kate said, glad of the scarf around her neck that hid most of her blush.

"Good."

"Why *good*?" Kate said, looking down at him, which felt distinctly odd, given how tall he was. There was a bright red bobble on the tip of his ski cap, just like Rudolph's shiny nose.

He shrugged. "Maybe you'll come with me instead?"

Kate opened her mouth and closed it again. She didn't have a clue what to say. Was he asking her for a date?

A real date?

She'd never gone on a date before, not even with Nathan. All they'd done was hang out together, and always with other people. Holly and Adam hadn't had a proper date yet, either—not like going out for pizza and ice cream or to the movies.

Brad waved his flashlight. "The party's gonna be at my house," he said. "No spiders this time. I promise."

* * *

By the time they reached the barn, Holly had already mustered the troops. Jennifer got busy rubbing Tapestry down, Robin bustled up with an armload of hay, and Sue added another bale of shavings to the already thick bedding in Tapestry's stall. An ambulance had taken Marcia to the hospital.

Wrapped in a clean horse blanket, Kate couldn't stop shivering. The warmest place was Liz's office, so she parked herself on a folding chair while Holly heated water in her mother's coffeemaker. She dumped it into a bucket of cold water.

"How's this?" she said.

Kate tested it with her fingers. "Good."

But when she dipped her foot in, she flinched. Like Brad warned, the water scalded her frozen toes, even though it was only lukewarm. Before leaving to retrieve his snowmobile, he'd given Kate his cell number and reminded her that she owed him an answer.

"What was *that* all about?" Holly said, the moment he disappeared. She grabbed the coffeepot and topped off the water in Kate's bucket.

Without thinking, Kate almost wrecked Adam's surprise. "He asked me to—"

"Asked you what?"

"Nothing," Kate said, trying to wiggle her toes. "Just some stuff about frostbite."

It wasn't exactly a lie. Brad *had* cautioned against dunking her feet in hot water. As for the other stuff, she didn't know how to handle it. Was it okay to date two boys at once? Some of the girls at school did. Last week, Courtney boasted she'd gone out with three different guys from the football team, but that was probably just her showing off the way she always did.

"Liar," Holly said. "He's asked you out, hasn't he?" She gave Kate an odd look. "We're best friends. We share *everything*, right? So tell me."

Jennifer saved Kate from answering. She poked her head around the door and announced that Tapestry was all dried off. "I put a blanket on her. We gave her a little grain, some extra hay, and a bunch of carrots. She deserved a treat."

"Thanks," Kate said.

Her teammates clattered off down the aisle, talking excitedly about Kate's rescue mission and how brave she was, but all Kate felt was a sharp sense of guilt over leaving Tapestry in her stall for others to take care of. She tried to stand up, but her legs wobbled and gave out. Water slopped all over the floor.

Holly mopped it up, threw her wet towel in the corner, and plunked herself in another chair beside Kate. She looked about ready to jump on the Brad issue again when her mother raced through the door.

"Sorry I'm late," Liz said, breathing hard. "My truck got a flat, and—" She stared at Kate's bucket. "What happened here?"

"Frostbite," Holly said.

Her mother cringed. "That's nasty."

"It's not really frostbite," Kate said. "Just cold feet."

"*Seriously* cold," Holly said, grinning. "Brad Piretti wants—"

Kate gave her a sharp nudge. The last thing she wanted was a discussion about boyfriends and dating right now—at least, not till she'd figured it all out. Nathan's last text said he wouldn't be home until after Thanksgiving, maybe Christmas. And even then, he'd be in California and Kate would be … somewhere.

She had no idea where.

"How's Marcia?" Liz said. "Is she in the hospital? What about her mother? Did anyone get hold of Mrs. Dean?"

"I did," Holly said. "She sounded more annoyed with Marcia than worried about her."

"But Mrs. Dean went to the hospital, right?" Liz said.

Holly shrugged. "I guess."

"So, tell me what happened," Liz said, sinking into the swivel chair in front of her desk. Its wheels creaked ominously, like it was ready to collapse. "From the beginning, okay? Leave nothing out."

Taking turns, Kate and Holly gave Liz a detailed explanation. Kate didn't want to squeal on Marcia again, but she had to, otherwise Liz wouldn't fully understand why the girl had run off with her sister's horse. Liz nodded and said "hmmph" a few times, and her eyes widened when Kate described the evidence Marcia had found on her mother's front lawn.

"I'm sorry," Liz said, "for not believing you."

"That's all right," Kate said, feeling herself blush. She always got embarrassed when grownups apologized.

Liz stood up. "Time to get you home," she said, helping Kate to her feet. "Think you can hobble to my truck?"

Holly suggested Kate ride in a wheelbarrow. "On top of the manure I forgot to empty," she said.

They all laughed, but something in Holly's voice didn't ring true. She was clearly miffed that Kate hadn't confided in her about Brad, and she was obviously still suspicious over her clandestine texts with Adam. If Holly got any more teed off, Kate would have to blow holes in Adam's surprise. Otherwise, her friendship with Holly would blow up.

14

By NINE O'CLOCK, Kate's toes had returned to normal. She could walk from the kitchen to Holly's bedroom without wincing. Even her fingers had finally thawed out, and she was about to search Holly's laptop for her essay notes when there was a knock at the front door.

"I'll get it," Holly said, leaping off her bed. With Kate trailing behind, she raced for the living room and yanked open the door. Icicles fell off the gutter and shattered like glass all over the steps.

Kate did a double take. "Dad! What are you doing here?"

Ice and snow tumbled off Ben McGregor's shoulders as he pulled Kate into his arms. He hugged her so hard, she thought for sure her ribs would crack. His beard tickled her cheeks; his boots left puddles on the floor.

"Liz called me," he said. "Are you all right?"

"I'm fine, Dad. Really fine."

"She's a heroine," Liz said. "So's Tapestry."

"They're gonna make headlines," Holly said, grinning. "Trick Horse Lies Down in Snow to Save Frozen Teens from Coyotes."

Ben raised his eyebrows. "Really?"

"Yes, really," Liz said. "Just you wait till I tell you what your daughter and that mare did." With a smile, she waited while Kate's father stepped out of his boots and then ushered him toward the fire she'd just built.

Candles flickered on the mantel; a bottle of red wine and two glasses sat on the coffee table beside a bowl of peanuts. Kate hadn't noticed them on her mad dash for the door. And was it her imagination, or was Liz wearing makeup again? There was a touch of blush, a hint of eye shadow, and even her hair looked as if she'd spent more than five seconds brushing it. As for her father—well, apart from his mismatched socks, he was quite the poster boy for L.L. Bean in his hunter green turtleneck, plaid shirt, and neatly pressed khakis.

He settled into a chair with a glass of wine and asked Liz to tell him what had happened. As they talked, Holly curled up on the couch beside Kate and nudged her. "Remember what we said about getting our parents together?"

"Like buying them tickets for a cruise or the theater?"

"No, us running away together."

"But we didn't," Kate said. "We went looking for Marcia."

"Close enough," Holly said. "You got stranded, my mom called your dad in a panic, and it worked. Look."

Kate gulped. The whole *Parent Trap* thing was kind of ridiculous, but Holly was right about their parents. Sipping wine, they sat in matching armchairs on either side of the fireplace and gazed at each other like a couple of lovestruck teens. When did this happen? Had she missed something?

"I think they've been e-dating," Holly whispered. "Mom's been acting weird all week."

"Get real," Kate said. "They've only known each other for ten days."

"Phfft," Holly said, snapping her fingers. "That's plenty of time." She leaned closer. "Next up, the butterfly museum."

"What?"

"Don't be dense," Holly said. "Stage two, remember?"

"Yeah," Kate said, dubiously. She desperately wanted their crazy plan to work, but it'd go down the tubes if Marcia's evidence about Skywalker's shoe didn't hold water or if Kate didn't solve the plagiarism issue at school. Her notes had to be on Holly's computer.

They *had* to be.

* * *

After much searching, Kate found her notes in an untitled folder buried inside Holly's collection of horse photos. Who knew how they got there? With a feeling of relief, Kate zipped up her files and e-mailed them to Ms. Tucker.

Holly said, "I bet Angela did this."

"But how?" Kate said. "It's impossible."

They'd looked it up online. The site for ferreting out plagiarism was used by lots of schools besides theirs. Its algorithms flagged chunks of text that matched others. No way could it have found a match for Kate's essay, unless—

"Think," Holly said. "Who had access to your file?"

"You," Kate said.

Holly threw a pillow at her. "Where did you go right before giving Ms. Tucker your essay?" she said, sounding like *Harriet the Spy*.

"The computer lab," Kate said. "I made some last-minute changes."

"Did you copy your file to the computer?"

Kate thought for a moment. "Yes."

"And did you trash it afterward?" Holly said.

"I think so," Kate said, backpedaling madly. She couldn't really remember. Holly would crawl all over her if she admitted to not deleting her essay from the school's computer system.

"Okay," Holly said. "Who else was there?"

It was only three days ago, but it felt like three weeks. Kate reversed her mental clock and saw Angela's flash drive dangling from its neon pink ribbon, swinging back and forth as Angela demanded the computer that Kate was using.

"Well?" Holly prompted.

Kate felt sick. "Angela."

"I knew it," Holly said. "You forgot to delete your file, and Angela found it after you left and figured out another way to slam you by sending it to the validation site." She let out a low whistle. "If I didn't hate her so much, I'd be impressed." There was a pause. "You've gotta tell Ms. Tucker."

"No," Kate said. "My notes will prove I didn't do it. I'm not going to—"

"Squeal?" Holly said.

Miserably, Kate nodded.

"Why not?" Holly said, almost shouting. "Angela would squeal on *you* in a heartbeat."

"I am *not* Angela," Kate said. "And we have no proof."

"You always say that, but—"

Kate waved her off. It wasn't enough to insist you were innocent and hope that people believed you, especially when it came to teachers in a brand new school. She had no track record at Winfield High; she was still the new kid on the block. Besides, nobody liked squealers. They always ended up smelling worse than the people they were squealing on.

"I'll figure it out, okay?" she said.

Her father stuck his head around the door. "I'm off to Aunt Marion's," he said. "I'll check in with you tomorrow."

Kate kissed him goodnight. They hadn't talked about his trip to New York or why things hadn't worked out down there. She'd asked him about it more than once, but he'd sidestepped her questions. He'd been totally focused on her and Tapestry and their dramatic rescue mission; he'd also been totally focused on Liz.

Maybe Holly was right.

Maybe there *was* something going on.

* * *

Kate was in line at the cafeteria when the PA system summoned her to the principal's office for the second time in two months. She flinched as if someone had slapped her.

This was it.

Ms. Tucker had decided her notes were bogus, and she was about to be suspended. Her tray wobbled. The chicken salad she'd just pulled from the cooler slid to one side, and only Holly's quick reaction saved it from splattering all over the floor.

"Don't forget what I said," Holly whispered. "Stand up for yourself." She took Kate's tray. "I'll save you a seat."

"Don't bother," Kate said. "I probably won't be back."

Miserably, she trudged toward Mrs. Gordon's office. Classmates raced past, shrieking and shoving each other like exuberant puppies without a care in the world. The school secretary held the door open and told Kate to go right in.

From behind her desk, Mrs. Gordon flashed a toothy smile. With her was a man Kate didn't know, yet she had a funny feeling she'd seen him before, or someone just like him.

"This is Henry Dean," the principal said.

Marcia's dad?

Kate had never met him, but the connection was obvious. His wavy red hair and brown eyes were a dead giveaway, along with the freckles that marched across his nose the way Marcia's did.

"Thank you for saving my little girl," he said, grasping Kate's hand.

Wearing a pinstriped suit, highly polished shoes, and a silky blue tie, Marcia's father looked as if he'd just been chauffeured straight up from Wall Street or wherever it was that businessmen worked. Kate glanced out the window, half expecting to see a stretch limo parked at the curb.

"I'll give you some privacy," said Mrs. Gordon.

Quietly, she slipped from the room but left the door partway open. Through the gap, Kate could see her bending over the secretary's desk, pointing at something on her computer screen.

"Is Marcia all right?" Kate said. "I mean, is she—?"

"She's going to be fine, thanks to you."

"It wasn't just me," Kate said. "Holly's the one who rode for help and told the Pirettis where to find us."

"Oh," he said. "Marcia didn't tell me."

"She was pretty much out of it," Kate said, remembering Marcia's white face and terrified eyes. "She probably didn't even realize Holly was there."

Mr. Dean nodded toward the door. "Maybe Mrs. Gordon could get Holly in here. I'd like to thank her as well."

Kate hesitated. If Holly heard her name on the PA, she'd panic and think Kate had flipped out. She'd probably swoop into Mrs. Gordon's office like a Valkyrie, ready to defend Kate with her sword. Besides, Holly hated it when people made a fuss of thanking her. "She's in the middle of a make-up test," Kate said, hoping Holly wouldn't kill her for lying. "So—"

"Then we won't disturb her," Mr. Dean said. "But will you thank her for me? Tell her how grateful I am?"

"Sure," Kate said.

He pulled out his wallet. For an embarrassing moment, Kate thought he was about to give her money, but he handed her a couple of business cards instead. "If there's ever anything I can do for you, or Holly, promise to let me know," he said.

"Yeah, okay," Kate said, shoving his cards in her pocket. "How long will Marcia be in the hospital?" The bigger question she didn't want to ask was, *How would Marcia be able to live with her stepmother after this?*

As if he sensed her unspoken concern, Henry Dean said, "I'm taking my daughter back to New York later this afternoon. I've already enrolled her in a private school."

"New York?" Kate said. "But there aren't any stables in Manhattan, not for kids like Marcia." The only one Kate knew of was for volunteers who patrolled Central Park on horseback.

Marcia's father smiled—a genuine smile that lit up

his pale face. "There are plenty of top-rate training barns in Connecticut and on Long Island," he said. "Don't worry, I'll find somewhere for her to ride—every week-end."

"Marcia's good," Kate said, meaning it.

Mr. Dean smiled again. "That's what she tells me," he said. "And she really loves your horse. Can't stop talking about her. So if you ever decide to sell—"

Kate shook her head. "Tapestry's not for sale."

"Fair enough," he said, shaking Kate's hand again. "I can't thank you enough for everything you've done for my little girl. Not just rescuing her, which was amazing, but for taking the time to help with her riding and to listen to her. I really appreciate it. More than you know."

"She's a nice kid," Kate said.

He gave an embarrassed cough. "About my wife's front lawn. Marcia told me what happened, and I'd like to apologize for—" A blush spread up his cheeks, and Kate felt kind of bad for him. It wasn't *his* daughter whose dirty tricks had caused so much trouble. "I'll see that it gets taken care of, along with a few other things," he said.

"Thanks," Kate said, with a sigh of relief.

One problem solved; only a couple more to go. Maybe he'd like to wave his magic wand over her essay disaster and make that go away, too. And while he was at it, perhaps he could persuade her father that they really did need to live in Vermont.

"I'm sorry for interrupting your lunch break," Mr. Dean said. "I hope you didn't think you were in trouble." He gave a wry grin. "That PA system is enough to scare anyone. I used to be terrified of it, even when I hadn't done anything wrong."

There was a soft knock on the door.

Mrs. Gordon poked her head around it. "Kate, when you're through here, Ms. Tucker wants to see you."

"She's a popular girl," Henry Dean said.

Hardly, Kate thought. More like a pariah.

15

FEET DRAGGING LIKE SANDBAGS, Kate climbed the stairs to Ms. Tucker's office. Maybe Holly was right. Maybe she ought to squeal on Angela if her notes didn't do the trick. She was tired of being the good girl who never made a fuss. This time, she'd stand up for herself, even if—

Kate swallowed hard and knocked on the door.

It opened, and Ms. Tucker waved her into a chair. She handed Kate a fresh printout of her essay and Kate hardly dared to look. Through scrunched-up eyes she made out a big red *A* at the top and the words *Well done* scrawled in the margin.

"Your notes proved this is your work," Ms. Tucker said. "So you can stop worrying."

Kate wanted to punch the air with her fists. She

didn't want to cry—not again—but the tears came anyway, great big ones filled with a giddy sense of relief that she wouldn't have to risk blowing the whistle on Angela.

"I'm sorry," she said, sniffing. It seemed as if all she'd done in front of this teacher was bawl her eyes out.

"Don't apologize," Ms. Tucker said, handing her a tissue.

Kate blew her nose. "Thanks."

"We can't explain what happened with your essay," Ms. Tucker went on. "It could've been a software glitch or server problems. But we've also heard reports from other schools about students gaming the system, so we're keeping a sharp lookout for it here."

For a moment, they looked at one another in silence, and Kate got the distinct impression Ms. Tucker knew more about this than she was willing to admit.

Had someone squealed on Angela?

* * *

"Duh, uh," Holly said, when Kate filled her in. "It was Marcia, you idiot. That's obvious. I mean, who else could it be?"

"You?" Kate said, grinning.

Holly rolled her eyes, but the more Kate thought about it, the more sense it made. Marcia was brilliant at appearing without warning. She'd learned to keep a low profile at home and probably heard all sorts of things she wasn't supposed to hear, like Angela boasting to Courtney how she'd gotten her own back at Kate McGregor by feeding her essay to the validation site.

If so, had Marcia told anyone else?

She hadn't told Kate, but maybe she'd confided in her father and he'd passed it along to Mrs. Gordon before she summoned Kate to her office. There would've been plenty of time for the principal to give Ms. Tucker a heads-up that Angela was making it look as if Kate had cheated. Kate gave a little sigh. This was turning into a *Nancy Drew* novel.

Holly said, "I bet Angela will get suspended."

"Dream on," Kate said, as they climbed onto the bus.

Angela never got punished. She never had to face consequences, no matter how badly she behaved. Her mother made sure of that. Mrs. Dean was head of the school board and president of the PTA.

Her busy fingers were everywhere.

* * *

When they got home, Liz took Holly for a dental checkup and Kate headed toward the barn. For once, she had the place to herself. Robin and Sue were at soccer practice, Angela was flourishing pom-poms in the gym,

162

and Jennifer had gone cross-country skiing. She said the conditions were perfect.

Horses whickered as Kate raced down the aisle. Rakes, pitchforks, and brooms hung from metal hooks between stalls; empty muck buckets in a rainbow of colors waited to be filled. Everything was comfortable and familiar. Kate scooped a stray hoof pick off the floor, dropped it in her pocket, and followed one of the barn's feral cats into the tack room. The tabby scrambled out of sight behind a pile of blankets.

Reaching for her saddle, Kate wondered how many more times she'd get to pluck it off this old wooden rack that had Tapestry's name engraved on a small brass plaque beneath it. How much longer did they have together before her father's job sent them who knew where? He hadn't talked about it, but Kate knew it was coming.

Tonight, probably.

She grabbed her grooming box and ran back to Tapestry's stall, fed her a couple of carrots, and got busy with brushes and a currycomb. There was too much snow to ride outside, so Kate tacked up her horse and headed for the indoor arena. The last class to use it had left a course of jumps around the perimeter that looked inviting, but first she needed to warm up.

Tapestry arched her neck and jigged in place, showing no signs of fatigue from the previous night's adventure. She took short, choppy strides and skittered sideways around an orange traffic cone. Today, obviously, the cone had horse-munching teeth.

Kate laughed out loud.

Robin once that said horses were afraid of only two things: *things that moved* and *things that didn't*. Still laughing, Kate gathered up her reins and asked Tapestry for a steady, flat-footed walk, but Tapestry wasn't interested in walking. She wanted to run. She wanted to erupt like a two-year-old Thoroughbred and snort at stuff she'd seen a million times before. It took thirty minutes of half-halts, circles, and patient schooling before the mare was ready to jump.

She flew over the course like a golden eagle.

Somebody clapped.

Astonished, Kate turned toward the observation room. Her father waved and then clapped again. With a smile, he stepped into the arena and walked toward her, giving her a double thumbs-up.

"That looked great," he said.

Kate shrugged. "It was okay."

She'd mistimed the last two fences, but only another rider would've noticed. Still, it was nice to hear Dad dishing out compliments, especially about her horse.

Patting Tapestry's neck, he said, "I saw Dr. Zimmerman in New York, and—"

"*Doctor?*" Kate said, alarmed. "Are you okay?"

"I'm fine," he said. "I'm talking about Reuben Zimmerman, my old professor. He's friends with your principal, and apparently they both think I should buy—"

Tapestry whinnied. Kate whipped around and saw Holly riding Magician into the arena.

"—the butterfly museum," her father finished, so softly Kate barely heard him.

"What did you say?" she said, hardly daring to breathe.

He gave her a shy smile. "The butterfly museum. How would you feel about us owning Dancing Wings?"

"I'd love it!" Kate shrieked. She leaped off Tapestry's back and flung both arms around her surprised father. He staggered backward. Kate let go and looked at Holly, looming above her on Magician.

"Told you," she said, giving Kate a high five.

Kate's father said, "Don't get too excited, because I don't know if I have enough money to pull it off. We'll need help with funding, and a place to live, and—"

"We've got Aunt Marion's cottage," Kate reminded him, rummaging through her pockets. Her fingers bypassed the hoof pick and closed around the crisp edges of Mr. Dean's business card. She pulled it out and read the words beneath his embossed name: *We invest in small business.*

With a big smile, she gave it to her father.

* * *

There was no sign of Angela at school the next day. Courtney spread it about that her cousin had the flu. "She's got to get better by Saturday," she said, with a pout. "We've got a big game, and the guys can't win unless we cheer them on."

"Yeah, right," Brad Piretti muttered.

He winked at Kate and lumbered past, footballs cleats clattering on the tiles and shoulder pads bulging beneath his green-and-yellow jersey.

Kate still hadn't given him an answer about Holly's party. She had too many other amazing things to think about, like moving to Vermont and Dad buying the butterfly museum. With one phone call, Mr. Dean had set the ball in motion. He'd promised that Ben McGregor would get the financing he needed.

Holly called it the best revenge ever.

Angela's stepfather was making sure that Kate and Tapestry would stay at Timber Ridge.

Permanently.

Don't miss **Book 6** in the exciting
Timber Ridge Riders series,
coming in June, 2013

Almost Perfect

KATE MCGREGOR and her best friend Holly
Chapman share the same dream. They want to
qualify for the annual Festival of Horses where
scouts from the United States Equestrian Team
will be on the lookout for promising young
riders.

Goaded by her relentless mother, Angela
Dean has the same dream, which means the
girls are locked in a fierce competition to de-
termine who will represent Timber Ridge at
the next qualifying horse show. But when Mrs.
Dean sticks her finger in the pie, Kate's dream
takes an unexpected tumble.

To make matters worse, Angela's new best
friend is moving to Timber Ridge and she can't
wait to join Angela's vendetta against Kate.
Except that now, Angela's got her claws into
Holly as well.

Sign up for our mailing list and be among the first to know when the next Timber Ridge Riders book will be out.

Send your email address to:
timberridgeriders@gmail.com

For more information about the series, visit:
www.timberridgeriders.com

Note: all email addresses are kept strictly confidential

About the Author

MAGGIE DANA'S FIRST RIDING LESSON, at the age of five, was less than wonderful. She hated it so much, she didn't try again for another three years. But all it took was the right horse and the right instructor and she was hooked.

After that, Maggie begged for her own pony and was lucky enough to get one. Smoky was a black New Forest pony who loved to eat vanilla pudding and drink tea, and he became her constant companion. Maggie even rode him to school one day and tethered him to the bicycle rack ... but not for long because all the other kids wanted pony rides, much to their teachers' dismay.

Maggie and Smoky competed in Pony Club trials and won several ribbons. But mostly, they had fun—trail riding and hanging out with other horse-crazy girls. At horse camp, Maggie and her teammates spent one night sleeping in the barn, except they didn't get much sleep because the horses snored. The next morning, everyone was tired and cranky, especially when told to jump without stirrups.

Born and raised in England, Maggie now makes her home on the Connecticut shoreline. When not mucking stalls or grooming shaggy ponies, Maggie enjoys spending time with her family and writing the next book in her TIMBER RIDGE RIDERS series.